THE COST OF INNOCENCE

THE COST
OF INNOCENCE

Jeffrey Ashford

SEVERN
SH
HOUSE

This first world edition published in Great Britain 1998 by
SEVERN HOUSE PUBLISHERS LTD of
9–15 High Street, Sutton, Surrey SM1 1DF.
This first world edition published in the U.S.A. 1998 by
SEVERN HOUSE PUBLISHERS INC of
595 Madison Avenue, New York, N.Y. 10022.

British Library Cataloguing in Publication Data

Ashford, Jeffrey, 1926-
        The cost of innocence
        1.   Hit-and-run drivers - Fiction
        2.   Suspense fiction
        I.   Title
        823.9'14 [F]

        ISBN 0-7278-2211-X

Typeset by Hewer Text Ltd,
Edinburgh, Scotland.
Printed and bound in Great Britain by
MPG Books Ltd, Bodmin, Cornwall.

One

W hen the weather was reasonable, Ryan walked to and from the office since exercise was said to be almost as good for one's well-being as a glass or two of red wine. As he turned into Yarrow Lane, the many angled slate roof of Ragstone Hall became visible, offering a sharp contrast to the tiled roofs of the houses on either side. He yet again regretted, though did not resent, the fact that Laura did not share his love for their home. True, it was by modern standards overlarge, ungainly, and difficult to maintain, yet it had been built for his great-great-grandfather. But maybe romantic nostalgia always took a back seat when it became a question of keeping many large rooms clean and coping with the sudden domestic crises that ancient plumbing and wiring provoked . . .

When built, green fields had surrounded Ragstone Hall; now, thanks to a great-grandfather who had gambled and successive rapacious governments, the fields had been replaced by suburban housing. The advance of mediocrity, the curse of the twentieth century. Within the past year, a developer had offered him just short of a million for the property because the garden was so large, but he'd turned down the offer, for once not discussing the decision with Laura. She would never have understood or accepted his refusal since the money would have enabled them to buy a very much more imposing house in the smart area of Amplestone. But had he accepted the offer, the house, the lawns, the flower beds, would have been replaced by more tasteless, boxy houses and links with his past would have been cut.

A man stepped out from the garden of the first house beyond Ragstone Hall and came towards Ryan, meeting him in front of the wider gateway in the eight foot high brick wall, only dimly illuminated because the nearest street light was some way away.

Ryan came to a stop. " 'Evening."

"Hullo, Mr Ryan. Just back from work? Been hard at it, then?"

Laura contemptuously referred to Tillett as a 'naff little erk'; this was cruel because his gauche manner was so obviously the result of nerves.

"For some time now, we've had to keep our noses to the grindstones. But I suppose we can't complain since solicitors in general are supposed to be going through lean times . . . How's the family?"

"We've just heard that Gwen has had a daughter. Eight and a half pounds. That's good, isn't it?"

"Very good," replied Ryan, hoping his ignorance of the quality of babies' weights was not obvious.

"Gwen's calling her Esmeralda. It means 'emerald' and apparently her eyes seem to be a bit green."

It was also the name of an unfortunate gypsy dancer. "Very attractive."

"Phyllis said we must wet her head. You wouldn't know if Sainsbury is still open, would you?"

"I'm afraid not."

"She said she was sure it would be, but she's all of a do over having a granddaughter. It's funny how women go soft over babies, isn't it?"

"Very." To his regret, Laura was an exception.

"Well, I'd better see if the place is still open. Don't you think their bubbly's a real good buy?"

"I do indeed. Give my best wishes to mother and new daughter."

"That's real kind of you."

They parted. Tillett to hurry along the pavement, Ryan to walk through the gateway into the yard. Facing him was the wing which originally had housed stables and feed rooms and, above, staff accommodation. One feed room and the stables had been converted into garages and in the former was Laura's Rover, in the latter was Keith Tyler's dark green BMW instead of his Astra shooting brake. As he continued past the dairy, scullery, kitchen, and pantry, he wondered why life was unfair enough to allow one to choose one's friends, but not one's relatives? A question to be forgotten. Although cousins, because they'd been brought up together when his parents were abroad, Laura and Keith were more like sister and brother – the kind that got on well together, that was. Any criticism of him always angered her.

Ryan turned the corner of the house which brought him to the gravel path that led from the entrance gateway to the front door. Beyond the path was a very large, well kept lawn, an elaborate fountain in which swam golden carp supposedly older than he, flower beds, and a belt of trees just inside the brick wall. With imagination, one could forget the boxy houses beyond them and return to green fields.

Three stone steps led up to a colonnaded porch with elaborate pediment; above the heavy, panelled wooden door was a fanlight with intricately fashioned glazing bars and stained glass depicting a scene difficult to specify; Laura said his great-great-grandfather had suffered from *la folie des grandeur*, he preferred to believe the old boy had had a sense of humour.

Jeffrey Ashford*

He unlocked the door and went into the hall – surprisingly modest – and hung his mackintosh and umbrella on the heavy mahogany coat-stand which had a stone base to catch any drips. From his left came the sounds of speech, the rhythm of which suggested television. He went into the sitting-room, only slightly smaller than the drawing-room. It had been furnished to Laura's taste, not his, and the conflict of styles had never ceased to irritate him. He crossed to the stripped pine settee, leaned over and kissed her on the cheek. "How are things?" he asked, as he straightened up.

She continued to look at the television. "The same as yesterday and the day before and the day before that."

"My father used to say, 'Lucky the man who returns in the evening to the home he left in the morning.' "

"Sounds as if he got that from a Christmas cracker."

Had his parents, who had valued the past, been alive when he'd met and married her, they would probably have silently disapproved. And his mother would surely have frequently considered Laura's dress highly inappropriate – decorum in all things were the hallmark of a lady. Yet wavy, chestnut brown hair, wide-apart eyes so deep a blue they could fire even a misogynist's interest, a retroussé nose, shapely, generous lips, a swan neck, and a body that went in and out at all the right places and to a fitting degree, meant Laura had the looks and figure to wear clothes that outlined and revealed . . . When he'd first met her, he'd known the sudden emotional shock that had a man wishing he were twice as handsome and ten years younger . . . "Where's Keith?"

She ignored the question, used the remote control to change channels. After a few seconds, she changed them again. "Nothing but repeats. Why the hell do we have to pay a hundred pounds a year to watch the same thing over and over again?"

4

"Ninety-seven pounds fifty."

"My God, how bloody typical! Must be absolutely and utterly precise."

"I'm afraid that's a spin-off from my job," he said lightly.

She switched the set off.

"I thought there was a programme on Tuesdays you liked watching?"

"It's become ridiculous. No one could lead the lives they're supposed to. Fiona met a man for the first time in the last episode and already he's given her a diamond bracelet that cost thirty thousand dollars."

It seemed her criticism was not based on artistic grounds. "If things are happening that quickly, you can bet that in the next episode she'll be supplanted by a redhead who'll be given a bracelet costing forty thousand."

"Must you be quite so facetious?"

He said quietly: "What's gone wrong?"

She swung her head round to stare at him. "What d'you mean?"

"You're obviously very fed up about something."

"I've got a thumping head."

"Oh! The usual?"

"No."

"Then what's caused it?"

"How the hell should I know?"

"Could it be your eyes?"

"No, it couldn't. And stop asking stupid questions."

He had learned to shrug off her bouts of bitchiness. "Hoping this is a sensible question, what would you like to drink?"

"A whisky and ginger," she answered ungraciously.

He walked the length of the room to the cocktail cabinet. Since this was in the form of a swags-decorated cabinet in Adam style, he had always considered it to be the room's ultimate anachronism. He poured out a whisky and ginger for her, a gin and tonic for himself; he handed her a glass, then sat in the second of four armchairs. "Is Keith upstairs?"

"Why d'you ask that?" Her voice was sharp.

He was surprised by her reaction to his question. "As he's not downstairs, I assumed he must be upstairs."

"He's not here."

"That is his car in my garage, isn't it?"

She spoke more calmly. "He rang this morning to say he was passing by and would call in to see me. Now, I suppose you're going to complain?"

"Why should I?"

"Because you so dislike him."

"I've told you time and again, I don't. It's just that I don't particularly like him, even though he's your cousin. It happens that way."

"That's lawyer's quibble. He told me after first meeting you that you made it very obvious you looked down on him because he spoke with an accent that marked him from the wrong background."

"He was talking nonsense. I don't give a damn what accent anyone speaks with."

"A dropped aitch has your upper lip hitting your nose."

It was ironic that it was she who judged people by meaningless social standards. "If I showed any emotion, it was surprise. After all, it's not every day that after being married for some years one is introduced to a hitherto unremarked relative."

"I told you, I'd never talked about him because he had been working abroad."

"Yes, but even so—"

"You will go on and on because you haven't the sensitivity to understand. I bet you can't remember asking me if he'd been in trouble with the law and then glutinously saying that even if he had, you wouldn't let that make the slightest difference to us."

The road to domestic misunderstanding was easily traversed. He'd been trying to lessen any sense of embarrassment she might feel.

"He was terribly upset by your behaviour."

He judged Keith too full of himself to be upset by someone else's opinions.

"You know what the truth is, don't you?"

"Tell me."

"You're jealous of him because he leads such an exciting life, travelling all the time while you just sit in your office."

"My immobility does have one great advantage. It lessens the chances of being murdered by a fundamentalist."

"Security! That's all you ever think about."

It wasn't the first time that he'd noticed a visit from Keith seemed to make her discontented. "I know it makes his life sound very glamorous, but it's probably not all that wonderful in fact. Fast cars, luxury hotels, and alluring women don't always—"

"Why mention them?"

"They are a natural consequence of an overfilled wallet."

"So that's why you dislike him!"

"My choice is monogamy with you." He hoped he sounded more convinced than just for the moment he perhaps was. He changed the conversation. "You haven't said why his car is in the garage and mine isn't. Has he made a straight swop?"

"God, your sense of humour!" She'd never understood that even a dismal sense of humour could act as a shield. "If you really want to know, on his way here the engine didn't seem to be running quite as smoothly as it should and as there are local BMW agents in town, he decided to get them to make

7

a quick check. Then he had a call on the mobile to say he had to meet someone for dinner in Randers Cross. It's an impossible journey by train as it's cross-country, so he said he'd call a taxi. I told him to borrow the Astra. I suppose if you'd been here, you'd have refused to lend it to him."

"On the contrary. All I'd have said would have been, please don't drive it as you do your own projectile."

"He's a much better driver than you."

"Probably not very difficult. Presumably, he's returning later on and spending the night here?"

"Do you object?"

"Far from it."

"That makes a change!"

He finished his drink. "How about the other half?"

"Two drinks before dinner! My God! The excitement is giving me palpitations."

Two

In the smaller of the two squares in Randers Cross, there stood a statue of Sir John Slight. In the latter part of the nineteenth century, he'd made a fortune from exploiting labour; then, in truly Victorian style, had used a tithe of that fortune to ensure he died a noted philanthropist. Facing this statue was the Alouette. Originally The Welcome Caff, it had been bought by a man who had decided to turn it into a restaurant of renown. In pursuit of this aim, he had observed the three essentials for success – he bribed a good chef to work for him, set the menu prices far higher than could be economically warranted and sent a case of *premier cru* wine to every noted writer who had a column on food and drink in an upmarket magazine or broadsheet.

The two men who sat at the right-hand table by the far window could hardly have been more different in appearance or character. Samaras had a shock of unruly black hair, a face sculptured in hard lines, eyes that were often focused on far distances, a complexion tanned by sun and wind, a very full beard, and a body built for physical work. Keith Tyler had styled hair, soft, handsome features, a complexion of which he took great care, and a slim figure. Samaras respected courage, Tyler, guile.

With a typical air of obsequious superiority, the wine waiter poured measures of Remy Martin into two balloon glasses that had been warmed, handed them over, left. Tyler said: "Then it's all systems go?"

"If the gods permit," Samaras replied.

"It's up to you to make certain they do."

Samaras shrugged his shoulders. "We have a saying, 'There is always one more possibility.'"

"You've more sayings than a dog has fleas."

"That is because we Greeks are an old race." He raised his left hand and looked his wristwatch. "It will very soon be time to depart." He spoke English so fluently that it was only the occasional mispronunciation, the out-of-rhythm pause, or the slightly archaic use of words, that marked him a foreigner.

"What's the rush?"

"My plane leaves early in the morning."

"And it's still early in the evening. Drink up and have another cognac."

"Thank you, I have had enough."

"I thought seamen were meant to be good topers?"

"When I was a youngster, I would drink a tavern dry. Since then, I have learned that the subsequent pain is not worth the previous pleasure."

"I'm going to have another."

"A host's privilege."

"Change your mind?"

"Thank you, no."

"A stubborn bastard."

"Perhaps."

Tyler drained his glass, then snapped his fingers. The wine waiter, masking his resentment at being summoned like a skivvy, took the order.

Tyler played with his empty glass, twisting it around with thumb and forefinger. "You've checked all the figures and times with Aristides?"

10

"Of course."

"And everything's running smoothly?"

"So far."

The wine waiter returned with two glasses and began to pour.

"Not for me, thank you," Samaras said, before the second glass could be used.

"So don't try putting it down on the bill." Tyler chuckled.

As the wine waiter turned away, he finally allowed his contempt to show. Tyler drank. "This is a bit different from the stuff in your country. That all tastes like horse piss."

"Our wines and spirits are perhaps an acquired taste."

"And if you've any sort of a palate, you take care not to acquire 'em. How about a cigar?"

"Thank you, but I do not smoke."

"No real drinking, no smoking; what about women? Or are you practising to be a monk?"

"I imagine a cowl would not fit me."

Tyler called to the nearest waiter to bring a cigar. A second waiter arrived with three open boxes. Tyler chose a cigar and it was cut, then a non-safety match was struck for him. He drew on the cigar, lazily exhaled. "I'll bet you've no idea how hard it's been to get things set up."

"I make certain I know only what I need to know."

Tyler leaned back in his chair. "You're a miser. Never give anything away, especially about yourself."

"A man should be a closed book to everyone but himself and only if he is strong enough should he try to open the pages."

"I suppose that's another Greek saying?"

"More likely, in origin it is Turkish, since it is very pretentious and rather stupid . . . Keith, I must leave."

11

"Why are you really in such a hurry? A blonde? Or a pair of blondes, waiting at the hotel? Confess."

"I confess that at my age, two would be too many."

"You expect me to believe you can't still make the bed thump The Galloping Major?"

"For tonight, all I wish for my bed is that it remains flat calm. Now, if we could leave?"

Tyler called for the bill. When it was brought, he studied it. "You have to check the bastards don't take you for a ride . . . And to begin with, we haven't had two bottles of wine!"

"We started with a white and then had a red."

"Did we? Damned if I can remember . . . Tell you one thing. With the prices they've the nerve to charge, the owner has a couple of Ferraris in the garage. Bloody thief." Tyler was beginning to slur his words. He laughed, so loudly that he drew the attention of other diners. "But pretty soon, it won't matter—"

"Enough."

Samaras had spoken quietly, but with such force that Tyler was silent for several seconds before he said resentfully: "I was only going to say—"

"Say nothing and pay the bill."

"There's no need to act like you're strutting about on your boat."

"Ship."

"Boat, ship, what the hell?" He brought a wallet out of his inside pocket and extracted several notes which he put down on the plate on which the bill had been brought. When the waiter picked up the plate, his thanks made it clear that he considered the tip to be mean.

They left the restaurant and walked across the square past Sir John Slight, whose face revealed more of his true character than he would have wished, to the parked Astra. Tyler had trouble finding the key and then in bringing it out of his trouser pocket. He pressed the key button to unlock the car. "The old banger isn't mine. I've recently bought the latest BMW."

"So you said earlier." Samaras pulled open the front passenger door and climbed in.

Tyler settled behind the wheel and had difficulty in inserting the key in the ignition lock.

"Perhaps it would be best if I drive to the hotel?" Samaras said.

"Are you suggesting I've had too much to drink?"

"Yes."

"I could drive a straighter line than you if I'd drunk twice as much. The Greeks are the worst drivers in Europe."

"Only when they're sober."

Tyler started the engine, engaged reverse gear, let out the clutch and the engine stalled.

"The handbrake is still on," Samaras observed.

Furious, Tyler restarted the engine.

"Drive slowly."

He released the handbrake. "Do I tell you how to sail your bloody boat?" He backed, turned, drove up the high street.

The old part of town was a maze of narrow roads. Tyler, who prided himself on his sense of direction almost as much as on his brilliance as a driver, only accepted he'd lost his way when they turned into a cul-de-sac. He swore, convinced Samaras would be silently laughing at him. He turned too sharply and the rear right-hand tyre clipped the kerb, jolting them. Infuriated, he accelerated and the car mounted the other pavement with a thump.

"It is your good fortune that this is not your car," Samaras observed.

Tyler raced up to the corner and turned left with a squeal of tyres, then left again. Immediately around the second corner, a car had parked facing the wrong direction and a woman was climbing out of the left-hand front seat. Reactions dulled, he neither swerved nor braked in time; the nearside front wing of the Astra struck the woman and flung her forward into the opened door.

Instinctively, he now braked heavily.

"Drive on, as fast as possible," Samaras said sharply.

Tyler once more accelerated.

Three

Tyler turned into the lay-by, separated from the road by a band of trees around the bases of which was thick undergrowth.

"What have you stopped for?" Samaras demanded.

"I need to think."

"You needed to do that back there."

Tyler was surprised how calmly and coherently he could now think. He switched off the lights and the engine.

"In the name of God," Samaras said in exasperated tones, "now what?"

"I have to check the car."

"You have to get right away from the town. If the police catch up with us, they'll want to know who I am and they'll ask why I'm in this country and not with my ship."

"Unless someone got our registration number, we've time to play with — and the odds are against that since there was no one else in the road and the people around the car looked too old to have their wits about 'em. Open the glove locker and see if there's a torch inside."

"There is," Samaras said after a moment.

"There are advantages to a man who carefully foresees every possible emergency . . . Let's be having it."

Samaras handed a small torch across. "What d'you want it for?"

"To see how things look."

Tyler left the car and walked round to the front, switched on the torch. "Shit!" he said aloud. Until then, he'd assured himself that because he'd only heard a dull thump at the time of the collision, a body was a yielding surface, and they had not touched the parked car, the Astra would have suffered no noticeable damage.

He returned to his seat, handed the torch to Samaras to replace, put his hands on the wheel and began to tap with his fingers.

"What are you waiting for?"

"The nearside headlight's been broken and probably the surrounding metal has been rippled; there could be a pattern on the paintwork. There'll certainly be glass on the road."

"What if there is?"

"You don't know much about police work."

"I've certainly not had your experience."

"There's some born honest, but not many." He began to tap more quickly. "What sort of profile will this case carry? Depends to some extent on how badly hurt she is, but in that neighbourhood she can't count for anything. So if the police have no more than some broken glass and a mark or two on her, they won't waste their time. That's the optimistic scenario. Now the pessimistic one. Somehow, they get a much stronger picture of the car and even track it to the sainted Alan . . . This car has to be very quickly, very quietly repaired." He took his hands off the steering wheel, turned the ignition key to start the engine, switched on the lights, engaged first, released the handbrake, and drove forward, halting at the exit to the lay-by to allow an oncoming lorry to pass.

As he drew on to the road, Samaras said: "Now what happens?"

"You can stop thinking you can hear the sounds of

handcuffs – I'm dropping you close by your hotel. Then the car's going to a man who's so smart he can nick your old banger and sell it back to you as new."

Burrell stepped out of the CID Escort and pulled up the collar of his bomber jacket to keep the light drizzle at bay. He crossed to where a uniform PC stood by one of the traffic cones which surrounded the Peugeot.

"So how's yourself?" the PC asked cheerfully.

Morosely, Burrell interpreted the other's question as derisive. Ever since his wife had left him, he'd been convinced he was the butt of endless scorn. Within the force, departing wives were relatively commonplace, but Helen had left with another woman. "The victim's gone, has she?"

"The ambulance took Mrs Yates off not so long ago."

"What state's she in?"

"The paramedic reckons it's broken bones and internal injuries; could be touch and go whether she survives."

Burrell stared at the Peugeot, the top of which was spotted with pricks of light as raindrops reflected the nearest street lamp. You never knew, he thought. He'd arrived home looking forward to some hot grub and had found an icy note . . "Are there any traces?"

"Bits of glass on the road which must be from the hit-and-run, but nothing on the Peugeot because it was only her body hit that. Might be something on the woman's clothes."

"Has the hospital been asked to store them very carefully so they can't be contaminated?"

"Sure."

"What's the story?"

"Hard to tell much. Yates is too shocked to help, Mrs Green didn't realise what was happening until it had happened. Like

17

everywhere, parking here is difficult and he turned into the first available spot after he'd passed his place; happened to be on his off-side. He and Mrs Green got out on to the pavement; Mrs Yates has a gammy leg and was taking her time. The hit-and-run came round the corner at speed and slammed her into the opened door."

"Do we have a description of the car?"

"Not so far."

"Any eyewitnesses amongst that lot?" Burrell indicated the knot of onlookers.

"I wouldn't know. Jim's been talking to them so you'll have to ask him."

"Which is the Yates' home?"

"Down the road on the other side. Number eighteen."

Burrell walked across to where the second PC was talking to an elderly man. As he approached, the PC said: "Right, Mr Fenn. Thanks for your help." When the latter was out of ear-shot, he said: "That old boy suffers from verbal diarrhoea."

"Is he any help?"

"As much as an empty glass."

Burrell stared at the onlookers. "Bloody ghouls, the lot of 'em."

"From ghoulies and ghosties and long-leggety beasties, Good Lord deliver us."

"How's that?"

"An old Cornish prayer."

"I'll just hang on to my goolies."

The PC was surprised by the attempted humour from a man recently nicknamed 'Mournful Meg'.

"Can any of 'em tell us anything?"

"Only the bloke to the right, in the mackintosh, and he's so sure of himself there's no saying how far to accept what he says."

"What does he say?"

"He'd returned home and was opening the door of his place – two down from here – when there was a squeal of tyres which made him turn. He saw a shooting brake driving real fast. He didn't see the impact because of the parked cars in the way of his line of sight and likewise he couldn't catch the number."

"What about make and colour?"

"Blue. No shadow of a doubt. Which means, it was likely pink."

Self-opinionated people could get things right, Burrell thought. A gust of wind swept along the road, driving the drizzle before it; he tried to snuggle deeper within the cover of the jacket's upturned collar. "And none of the others saw a thing?"

"They were all inside until they heard the screaming. By the time they came out, the car had vanished."

"Have another word with the one witness and find out if he sticks with the same story."

"Prove him wrong and he won't change it."

"All the same."

"Given up doing your own job, have you?"

Burrell checked the road was clear, crossed to the far pavement and walked along. He had lived in Randers Cross for the past twenty years and could remember when all the houses in the area had been slums. Then the local council, uncharacteristically finding out what people wanted instead of telling them, had not knocked everything flat and rebuilt, but had initiated a scheme to restore and modernise. Now there remained rows of terrace houses, with cat-swinging front gardens, but inside they were dry, warm, and comfortable.

Number 18 had a wooden gate and a small overhang to keep the worst of the weather off callers as they waited. He rang the bell. The door was opened by an elderly woman, her face plump and lined, dressed in clothes that owed everything to comfort and nothing to fashion. "Mrs Green?"

"That's me." She spoke with a slight accent which marked her as having been born in the North.

"Detective Constable Burrell, local CID."

"Come on in."

He stepped inside. On the right-hand wall of the entrance passage there hung a framed print of an elephant, trunk curled and held high. By bitter coincidence, Helen had bought a similar print and hung it in their dining-room. Life liked to kick a man when he was down . . .

"Would you come through?"

He jerked his thoughts back from the past and followed her into the front room, over-furnished with heavy pieces, spotlessly clean and tidy. "How's Mr Yates?"

"I gave him a couple of my sleeping pills and made him lie down and he's asleep. To tell the truth, I was getting ready to leave 'cause there's nothing more I can do here." She sat. "They told me there'd only be strife for Fred at the hospital 'til they knew how things was so he'd be much better at home . . . Have you heard anything?"

"I'm afraid not," he answered as he settled on the settee.

"She looked . . . well, like it was nasty."

"It's a wonder what medicine can do these days," he said, knowing his attempt to ease her distress was clumsy. "Will you tell me what happened?"

"We was at Bingo – Gwen's always liked to play and she's lucky. When we left, Alf suggested a quick one at the pub, but Gwen wanted to get back home so as Alf could have a beer and her and me a cup of tea. He saw somewhere to park and although Gwen said it was too far away, he said he'd better stop there or someone would come along and take it and he'd have to settle for another road and then it'd be even further to walk . . . If he'd gone round and dropped her and then looked again, this wouldn't have happened, would it?" Her expression was one of shocked strain.

"After every accident, Mrs Green, there's always an 'If only' to make one think like that. But the past can't be changed so it doesn't do any good."

She seemed to gain a measure of comfort from his naïve words. "I suppose that's right."

"Where were you sitting in the car?"

"Behind him."

"Which means you stepped out on to the pavement as he'd parked on the right-hand side. And Mrs Yates was slower getting out than you two?"

"She always took her time because of that leg. Only if she'd managed to move a bit quicker—" She sighed. "Like you just said, it don't do no good to say that."

"When did you first realise another car was coming round the corner?"

She spoke slowly as she concentrated in an effort to recall events accurately. She had been standing on the pavement and about to shut her door when a squeal of tyres had attracted her attention. She could remember thinking how erratically the car was moving. Instinct had prompted her to shout a warning to Gwen, now standing on the road, a hand on the opened door for support; events had moved too brutally quickly for Gwen to do anything. The oncoming car had thrown her against the open door; as she had dropped to the road, she had begun to scream. Those screams . . .

"It is terrible to hear such things," he said, unwillingly recalling screams he'd once heard. "Sorry to go on bothering you, but I do need to try to identify the car right away. Did you manage to note the registration number?"

21

"It was all so horrible . . . But when I saw it was going on, I tried to read the number."

"That was quick thinking."

"The trouble is, I wasn't wearing glasses because some years ago my sister had an accident in her car and bits of the lens was pushed into her eye. I suppose it's silly to worry the same thing could happen to me, but I do."

"You can never be too careful. You couldn't read the number plate, then?"

"Not really. I mean, my long sight's better than my short, but I was so upset everything seemed kind of blurred. But I think one of the letters was a P and one of the numbers was a six."

"How sure can you be?"

She hesitated, then said: "I just think."

"Can you say what kind of a car it was?"

She shook her head. "When I was young, they was different, now they all look the same."

"Was it a saloon, a hatchback, a shooting brake, or an off-road job?"

She hesitated. "It seemed like a saloon with a different back."

Confirmation it was a shooting brake? "What colour was it?"

"Dark." She paused, then added: "But I don't think it was black."

"Could you see who was in the car?"

"Only the passenger in the front."

"Can you describe the person?"

She spoke hesitantly and corrected herself once. In Burrell's mind, she pictured a large man, probably middle aged, with a strong face and a very full beard. "One last thing, whereabouts do you live?"

"Four roads away."

"Then I guess Mr Yates was going to run you home after the cup of tea?"

"That's right. I don't like being on the streets after dark these days. Things aren't what they used to be."

They never were. "I'll drive you back home."

Four

R yan was not surprised when Laura made a point of saying her head was no better as they entered the bedroom. Many husbands reported on the fact that the sight of bed seemed to induce or increase headaches in their wives.

They undressed in silence, climbed into bed. She offered him a perfunctory goodnight kiss, turned over and switched off her bedside light. He propped up his pillows, settled comfortably, picked up the paperback on the bedside table and opened it at the marker, but did not immediately read. What exactly had brought about her bitchy mood? It could not have been anything he'd said or done since he'd been away all day and when he'd left in the morning, she'd been very cheerful. Was she feeling ill? It would be unusual for her to conceal that fact. Had she had a row with Keith before he'd suddenly had to leave? Unlikely but not, of course, impossible. If there had been such a row, she would have been very upset. Could there be any other possible cause? He mentally shrugged his shoulders. It was easier for a politician to admit he was wrong than for a man to follow the mind of a woman.

He started to read and almost immediately was interrupted by the phone's ringing. As he reached for the receiver on his bedside table, Laura made a sound that suggested she had fallen asleep, but had been jerked half awake by the call.

"It's Keith. I thought I'd better ring despite the time

because otherwise the front door would remain unbarred and the alarms switched off and you'd not sleep soundly."

It always seemed to amuse the other that he took security so seriously.

"Things are very confused and I'm having to wait to meet someone who's on a plane that's been very badly delayed. I won't be back tomorrow and it could be even a couple of days after that because there'll be a lot more ground to cover than I reckoned when he eventually does get here. If you want a car, there's the BMW in the garage and the keys are in the ignition. You likely won't drive fast enough to realise the engine isn't a hundred per cent." He laughed. "Sorry about the chaos. I'll do penance. Love to Laura." He rang off.

"Who was that?" she mumbled.

"Keith."

"What's he want?"

"He won't be returning tonight and maybe not for a couple of days because someone he's meeting is coming in on a plane that's badly delayed and this seems to have confused things . . . I must go down and lock up."

He made his way downstairs. There, he shot home the bolts on the front door and switched on the downstairs alarm system, which had a two minute pause before it became active. Back in their bedroom, he switched on the upstairs system.

"Did Keith say who he was meeting?" she asked, as he climbed into bed.

"A business acquaintance."

"Male or female?"

"I didn't ask."

"Because it's none of your business?"

"That's right."

"You're so damned predictable!"

There were many who'd have considered that an asset, not a disadvantage.

Five

If called upon to describe himself – something he would have tried hard to avoid – Detective Inspector Meyer might have spoken of ideals and dreams, but also of the ability to recognise that in the practical world there might be times when these had to be sidelined. In truth, despite all his experience, he was still reluctant even to acknowledge that the battle between good and evil was eternal and that the best good could hope for was never to lose. This reluctance meant that each time he saw justice mocked, he suffered a bitter anger. His wife had once told him he should have been born in a time when hair shirts were in fashion.

He looked up from his desk as Burrell entered.

"'Morning, sir." First greetings were usually formal. "The sarge said you wanted a word on the Yates case. I've just been on to the hospital and they say her condition is critical; the internal injuries were more serious than first thought."

"Sit down."

Burrell sat. He respected the DI, but resented the demands made on all those who worked under him.

"Is there anything to add to your report on the case?"

"Only that we've got the outer clothes she was wearing from the hospital. The coat's woollen and some of the fibres show signs of damage so that's likely the point of impact." Burrell then added, remembering Meyer's pernickety insistence that

29

nothing should ever be assumed without positive reason: "Of course, until we've matched heights and possible trajectories, we can't say any more than likely."

"Any sign of traces on the coat?"

"None I could see with a very casual check. I've left it to Forensic to look closely."

"The family friend . . ." He looked down at the typewritten sheet on the desk. "Mrs Green. Have you spoken to her again to see if she can come up with anything fresh?"

"No, I haven't."

"She was sharp enough to try to read the car's number, so maybe she can help more now she's had the time to remember. Have a word with her when you leave here."

"Yes. Only—"

"Well?"

"The sarge wants a witness statement p.b.q., and then I'm meeting a nark who swears blind he can offer a lead on the Branders Hill job."

"Tell someone else to get the witness statement."

"I don't think there is anyone else. Andy's at the course still, Bert's tied up court because the case is dragging, Greg and Norman are away with the flu and Ian's missus has just phoned through to say he looks like the bug's hit him."

"Sounds like a hospital casualty list . . . You'll just have to fit in the statement as and when you can."

"The sarge says it must be with A division by midday. It's needed in the Fallon case."

Priorities. As a newly sworn-in PC, Meyer had been dismayed when told by a sergeant on the point of retiring that the successful copper was the one who made certain he pleased his superiors, the efficient copper one who could sort out his priorities. After a measure of experience, Meyer had been forced to accept that there was truth in what the sergeant had said. Those promoted to higher ranks were not always the best at the job; because there was never sufficient manpower to meet all the demands made on it, to be in command called for a clear mind, an ability to compare values too dissimilar to be logically compared, and the acceptance that at times some crime must be disregarded . . . The Fallon case concerned a clever fraud, given considerable media cover, which had netted many thousands of pounds. Material loss could never be as serious as personal injury so that it would seem more important to identify the driver of the car which had injured Mrs Yates than to pursue the fraudster. But, however much he might emotionally reject the necessity, priorities had to be based on wider grounds. Because evidence in the Fallon case was strong, there was every chance of bringing it to a successful conclusion, to media approval; because there was so little relevant evidence in Mrs Yates's case, a prolonged investigation might well fail and even if it succeeded, the media was unlikely to report that success. Police forces were under mounting political and public pressure to be seen to succeed . . .

Burrell coughed and Meyer brought his thoughts back to the immediate present. "All right, you'll have to go for the statement. Speak to Mrs Green as soon as you can."

"Right, Guv."

"Have garages been circulated and asked for information on dark coloured shooting brakes brought in for repairs and the accessory shops for purchases of headlamp units?"

"Joe's been organising that."

Elliott never hesitated to explain that he'd work for the *Amplestone Gazette* only until he was approached by one of the London nationals. Had he not rated his abilities so highly, his ambition might have been more realistic.

31

He listened to Yates's mournful mumblings and reflected that a measure of emotional self-control made life much easier for other people. "Doctors are professional pessimists; makes 'em seem heroes when their patients get better."

"They say she's badly hurt inside."

There was no real story here, he reflected. People were knocked down by cars every day of the week.

"It were awful, seeing her with them tubes and things in her and her not really knowing me—" Yates began to cry.

It was time to hurry things along. "You parked on the wrong side of the road so your wife had to get out on to the road?"

"She's got a bad leg."

"So you said. The car was skidding as it came round the corner?"

"Were it?"

"How fast d'you think it was travelling?"

"She couldn't get out of the way."

He'd call it sixty plus and use up a couple of lines to condemn drivers who used the streets as a race track. "I suppose the driver was tight?"

"I couldn't say."

As drunk as a pre-inflation lord. "And it just drove on?" Yates nodded as the tears rolled down his unshaven cheeks.

"You've no idea what kind of car or what its number was?"

He shook his head.

"That's about it, then."

"She were lovely." Yates brushed his cheeks with the back of his hand, then stood and reached across to the mantelpiece of the blocked-up fireplace on which were several photographs.

Realising what was about to happen, Elliott came to his feet. "I'll be off." He was too late. Yates picked up a photograph in a leather frame and held this out. "She were real lovely."

Elliott reluctantly took the photograph. It had obviously been taken decades before – Yates had all his hair and his wife, though far from beautiful, possessed a fresh attractiveness. About to hand the photograph back, his reporter's curiosity was suddenly caught. "What's she holding in her hand?"

"Her medal what the King had just given her; died soon after, he did."

"What kind of medal?"

"She didn't know what to wear. I mean, meeting the King—" He became silent with eyes unfocused as he retreated even deeper into the past.

"Why was she given a medal?"

"D'you want to see it?"

"I'd like to, yeah."

As Yates left the room, Elliott thought that perhaps he was going to find a worthwhile story after all.

Six

L ipman did not share Meyer's background, values, or somewhat sardonic acceptance of life's peculiarities. The detective sergeant, a graduate, was so self-confident that he seldom doubted himself and he possessed the kind of ambition which could wonder rationally what were the best means to employ to obtain high rank without any regard to the morality of these. Had he been less efficient, Meyer would have done his best to have him replaced by someone he found more congenial, less intellectually arrogant, and possessed of a broader sense of humour.

Lipman placed a typewritten list on the desk; Meyer picked it up and read the report on the night's assaults, robberies, drunk and disorderlies, and one attempted rape. He looked up. "What about Mrs Walters?"

"It's the fifth time in eight months that according to her someone's broken into her bedroom."

"You're treating it as one more false alarm?"

Lipman was sarcastically aware of the fact that if one made an assumption, one should never assume it was correct. "As doubtful. The WPC who spoke to her suggested she come to the special rape unit and have a medical, but she refused. However, I've told Greg to question her for form's sake."

Meyer thought, not for the first time, that Lipman was smoothness personified. Smooth appearance, smooth manner,

35

smooth superiority. Lipman was almost certainly correct in believing this report of rape to be a figment of the imagination, but it was a thousand pounds to a penny that he didn't look beyond that judgement to see a woman with a mind so troubled that she repeatedly claimed to have suffered what any untroubled mind most feared . . . "Greg's active again, then?"

"He's back and telling everyone he should still be on sick leave."

"I trust you praised him for his sense of duty?"

Lipman did not smile.

"What about Norman?"

"There's no sign of him as yet, but he went down with the flu a couple of days after Greg."

"Have we heard from Manchester yet?"

"I spoke to them yesterday evening and they promise the papers will be with us in the next couple of days."

"Anything on the Thompson boy?"

"His mother's had no word from him."

"And there's no hint of where he might have gone to?"

"Nothing."

"Can we be certain he disappeared voluntarily?"

"Quite certain, sir."

Meyer suspected Lipman often used the supposedly respectful 'sir' when he considered his superior was being thick. True, he had asked the same question only the morning before, but he could not overcome the thought of the mental hell the parents must be enduring and the physical hell the boy could be suffering if he'd fallen into the hands of one of the paedophile rings . . . "OK."

Lipman turned smartly and crossed to the door with quick strides, then said, hand on the door: "I suppose you read about Mrs Yates in the paper this morning?"

"No."

"There was a bit about her in *The Times*."

Lipman probably reckoned he read the *Sun*, Meyer thought sourly. In fact, he had the *Telegraph* every day but had not managed to look at it that morning before leaving home. "What's the reference?"

"The old girl won the George Medal when she was nineteen for defending two youngsters from a man high on drugs. Strange, isn't it?"

Strange that very ordinary people could be extraordinarily brave? "Have you got the paper here?"

"As a matter of fact, yes, I have."

"Let me see it."

Lipman left, to return within the minute. He passed the newspaper across. "Page three. There's a picture of the old girl after she'd received the medal. Looked a bit different then."

"Made weak by time and fate—" Meyer picked up the paper, opened it out, read. "This is going to give us the chance to dig a sight deeper." He put the paper down, settled back in the chair. "The case was low profile, now it can be high because she turns out to have been a teenage hero. There'll be media pressure to identify the driver, which means county will be pressing us to come up with a name, which means I'll be justified in using a lot more manpower."

"The odds against our succeeding will still be high."

"Is that any reason for not doing our damnedest?"

"Of course not, sir."

Meyer carefully folded the newspaper, handed it back. He had little doubt what was running through Lipman's mind. The greater the resources put into a case, the more success was demanded and the more failure was marked . . .

Lipman left. Meyer mentally considered the scant evidence there was. A dark coloured car, probably a shooting brake.

37

How many hundreds of thousands of vehicles on the roads did that description encompass? Some broken glass, almost certainly from the headlight. Could the magicians in the forensic laboratory conjure up any worthwhile details concerning the car from the slivers? An area on the coat which might mark where contact with the car had been made. Would any traces be found there? A registration number which might contain the letter P and the number 6 . . .

Should he put a request through to Swansea to ask them to provide a list of all dark coloured shooting brakes whose registration numbers included that letter and figure? To pose the question was to know the answer. Swansea charged for their work for the police on a commercial basis and therefore prior permission for its undertaking had to be gained from the detective chief superintendent – who had to consult the in-house auditor – if the bill was likely to be of any size. Here, the bill might obviously run into big figures and so permission would be refused and all the request would gain would be annoyance that it had ever been put.

It seemed that for the moment their only real hope of success was that the driver of the car lived reasonably locally and would identify himself by asking for his car to be repaired or by buying a headlamp unit. It was not an unreasonable hope. Ignoring motorways, the majority of accidents involved vehicles whose owners lived within twenty-five miles. But this hope had been with them from the beginning and so, contrary to what he'd said to Lipman, there was no immediate advantage to be gained from the fact that the case had become a high profile one . . .

"Damn," he said aloud, angry frustration providing the exclamation with the force it had once possessed, but had long since lost to other four letter words.

* * *

In the study, Ryan scrolled the image on the VDU as he read the draft will he'd just drawn up. Satisfied, he activated the printer. Wills were usually touched with regret since they spoke of death, this one was drenched in bile. What had the son done to arouse his mother's bitterness? When he had delicately asked the mother, hoping that as a neutral adviser he might persuade her it had to be wrong to disinherit one's only child except in the most extraordinary circumstances, she'd very bluntly said that that was none of his business . . .

He re-read the printed will. One could never be too certain. Even an 'and' in the wrong place could negate the testator's wishes since the lawyers' love of splitting legal hairs and confounding common sense had made the law concerning wills one of the most arcane. Finally satisfied, he put the draft in his briefcase, ready to be taken to the office and handed to a typist.

He yawned, looked at his wristwatch and was surprised to note how late the time was. Laura would be annoyed. For some reason he could never fathom, she resented his working at home at night, yet when he didn't and they were together, there was as likely to be silence as any conversation since she was a great television watcher.

He left the study and went along the passage to the hall. As he approached the sitting-room, it became clear that there was a visitor; before he opened the door, he identified Tyler's voice.

"One of the world's workers," Tyler said. "As someone less energetic, I salute you."

"In mockery, not respect?"

"Perish the possibility."

"In that case, I'll offer you a drink. What would you like?"

"A G and T, please."

Ryan turned to Laura. "You'll have the usual?"

"No, I won't, since I'm not you." Her tone was light. "I want a daiquiri."

"We've no limes left."

"That's where you're wrong again. I bought some this morning."

"Then a daiquiri you shall have."

She spoke to Tyler. "I've disturbed the rest of the evening for him, asking for something different."

"On the contrary, I'll bet you've given him the pleasurable spice of change. Isn't that so, Alan?"

"Indeed," Ryan replied. "Life has suddenly become twice as sharp."

"Don't you believe him," she said. "He's only happy when life is in a strait-jacket."

"There is something to be said for the *status quo*," Ryan observed. "Change can be for the worse as easily as for the better."

"And my choice of drink is a calamity in your eyes, isn't it?"

"Only if you proceed to have half a dozen. Then you'd be too woozy to get dinner."

Ryan went through to the kitchen, found the limes, poured the drinks. He opened a packet of garlic flavoured crisps and placed a handful in one glass dish, opened a tin of stuffed olives and emptied this into another. He carried everything through on a tray and as he handed Tyler a glass, said: "Did the plane eventually arrive?"

"What plane?"

"Weren't you meeting someone arriving on one that was badly delayed?"

Tyler said quickly: "Oh, him! He turned up eventually,

cursing aeroplanes and longing nostalgically for the traditional mail ship which arrived on the dot."

"Provided, of course, it didn't meet a heavy storm, fog, an iceberg, or run aground."

"Always the gloom merchant!" she said. "I'll swear you can think up a dozen disasters at the blink of an eyelid."

"I have the misfortune to be a realist."

"Hopefully I can bring a little good cheer back into proceedings, even for a realist," Tyler said. "As promised, I am doing penance for the disturbances in your life I've caused. There are half a dozen Veuve Clicquot in the boot of the Astra."

"That's so generous as to sound more an apology than penance."

"Why would I want to apologise?" Tyler said, no longer speaking with facetious good humour.

Ryan was surprised by the other's sudden change of tone. "Perhaps you've returned the car with tyres worn out because the only time you weren't doing a hundred was when you bothered to stop for red lights."

"If I'd managed to get your jalopy up to a hundred, I'd have brought a dozen bottles to celebrate having done the impossible!" Tyler's tone was once more bright. He drank. "So what do you think of a real car?"

"Presumably, you're referring to the BMW?"

"What else?"

"We only used it once to visit friends for dinner. They thought I must have suffered a brainstorm."

"Good taste always evokes jealousy."

"Or something. I must say, it seems quite fast."

" 'Quite fast'. Only a lawyer could be guilty of such stunning indifference to the sublime."

"When he's at the wheel, he's like an old arthritic," she

41

said. "On the way to that dinner we were on the M 25 and he suddenly found he was doing seventy-five. He panicked!"

"It wasn't the speed, *per se*," Ryan said. "It was the sight of a patrol car in the rear-view mirror."

"You know the police never stop anyone unless they're doing well over eighty."

"I know nothing of the sort. That's just one of those myths that people believe because everyone else believes them. The speed limit is seventy and if you do more than that, you're breaking the law."

"And you'd never, ever do such a terrible thing?"

"Not knowingly."

"Pass me the Brasso so I can polish your halo."

"Don't be too hard on him," Tyler said. "If there weren't any law-abiding people in this world, how would the rest of us get our pleasures from breaking the rules?"

She laughed.

When she could be bothered to take the trouble, Laura was a good cook.

"That," said Tyler, as he put down the teaspoon, "was easily the best chocolate mousse I have ever enjoyed."

"Flattery will get you nothing more," she said. "I only made enough for one portion each."

"How very inconsiderate."

"It's far too rich to have seconds."

"Why is it that the more desirable something is, the more reasons there are for not enjoying it?"

"Ask Ryan. He simply loves denial."

Tyler looked to the right of the candelabrum in which four scented candles were burning. "You can't believe that denial is good for the soul!"

"I suspect that sometimes it is."

"A perfectly ghastly suspicion."

She stood. "You two go on through while I get the coffee.

"Would people like a liqueur?" Ryan asked.

Tyler stood. "Thank God you're not a man to let your odd ideas ruin other people's pleasures! I'll have some of the magical Armagnac, if it's going."

A few moments later, Ryan and Tyler were seated in the drawing-room, each with a glass warming in his hand.

"So how have things been around here in the past few days?" Tyler asked casually.

"The same as ever."

"No alarums and excursions?"

"None that I know of. Why? D'you think there might have been something unusual happening?"

"Nothing specific, but these days pressure groups and do-gooders are around every corner, so you can't be certain."

Certain of what? Ryan wondered.

Seven

Divisional HQ seemed to have been designed by an architect who believed form to be all and content nothing. Seven stories high, it melded in surprisingly well with the old part of town which faced it on two sides; however, little attention had been paid to work patterns, an example of which disinterest was to be found in the distance between the charge-room and the cells – those escorting violent or drunk prisoners had good cause to curse the architect.

Meyer replaced the phone, stood, crossed to the large window and adjusted the Venetian blinds. It seemed absurd to shut out any of the sunlight since by the last day of October the sun was usually a stranger, but the room was already warm and stuffy, the window couldn't be opened, and the main air-conditioning unit was having one of its frequent sulks. He returned to his chair. Peggy had just rung in a panic because their son, who'd been sufficiently off-colour at breakfast not to go to school, was now feeling really rotten, but the surgery had said that a doctor couldn't call before midday; she'd been assured that the symptoms were not consistent with meningitis, but she was terrified that that was what Martin was suffering from since there was an outbreak in the West Country and what was she to do? He'd tried to calm her fears. Normally self-possessed, she panicked when either of the children was ill . . .

Burrell knocked and entered. "I'm just back from Thompson's Garage. False alarm. The car had a broken headlamp right enough, but I had a word with the owner who said he'd misjudged the entrance to his garage."

Meyer returned to his chair and sat. "Presumably, you checked out the possibility that he'd rammed something solid in order to obscure the damage caused by hitting Mrs Yates?"

"He and his missus say they were at their local until nearly eleven; the landlord backs 'em all the way."

"Were they tight when they left?"

"Probably, but no one's admitting it."

"Have any other reports come in?"

"No."

Burrell left. Time was working against them, Meyer thought. Garages and retail suppliers would soon forget there was a request to report. If the driver of the hit-and-run car kept it out of sight for long enough, he might well escape detection. Even the police might miss the significance of a dark coloured shooting brake which had had a headlamp replaced since minds could store and recall only so much information . . .

Lipman entered to stand just inside the door. "I've had a word with the hospital. Mrs Yates died at five-ten this morning."

"Poor sod!"

"She'd been unconscious for some time."

"The husband, Fred, the husband."

"Very sad for him, of course." He waited a moment, then left, closing the door behind himself.

Lipman was fortunate, Meyer thought; he seldom, if ever, vicariously suffered another's tragedy. He was well suited to high office.

Meyer stared at the map of the county on the far wall

without seeing it. Emotion should play no part in police work. Yet the knowledge that Mrs Yates had died made him even keener to identify the driver who, probably tight, had slammed her into the Peugeot's door. But bricks could not be made without clay, a case solved without facts.

Parker pinned a photograph on the noticeboard in the CID general room, used a red pencil to ring the head of the second man from the left, and wrote 'Who?'. He read, without any enthusiasm, a recently affixed circular promoting a dance, made his way to his desk. On it was a folder, attached to which with a paperclip was the note, 'Get this sorted out yesterday'. Lipman was a great man for rushing other people. Parker sat. How was he going to break down Hazel's resistance? It was disconcerting to find someone so old-fashioned that she didn't agree virginity denoted a lack of perspective. The phone rang.

"Forensic. The Yates case. We've classified the glass and will fax you the full details."

"As soon as you like."

"One more thing. The woollen coat had coloured dust at the point where contact was made. It's very fine and there's so little of it we can't carry out tests that would be meaningful in court; the best we can do is surmise it was paint dust raised by the force of impact and go on to say the car's colour is Prussian blue."

Parker thanked the other, rang off. Supposedly, the mixture of sun, sea, and sangria in Spain did wonders; might a bottle of plonk drunk on one of the local beaches lead to the same happy conclusion? . . . Was he bloody daft? It was the beginning of November and even if the sun appeared, the day would be cold enough to embarrass a man. In any case, Hazel never had more than one drink. Probably her mother had told her

47

it wasn't safe to enjoy a second one. Mothers could make for very grey skies.

He went down to the communications room and chatted to one of the civilian workers as he waited for the fax to come through. She was amusing, but reputably unavailable.

The fax was a mass of figures and abbreviations that would have taken him time to interpret, but thankfully all he was required to do was to transmit it through to NACVI – the national centre for vehicle identification – where were kept detailed specifications for every make and model of car produced.

It might have been months, not six days, since Meyer had adjusted the blinds to keep some of the sunshine out of his office. The sky was a dirty grey, the rain was steady, the wind was rising.

He studied the recently enumerated crime statistics for the past month and knew precisely how these would be received at county HQ. With sharp, but perhaps not openly expressed, annoyance and condemnation. Not just because crime in his division had risen and the clear-up rate fallen overall, but also because he lacked the wit to massage the figures so that the media might well gain the impression that crime had fallen and the clear-up rate had risen. His problem was his dislike of fudging. If challenged, he could explain precisely why the figures were as they were and why they didn't discredit divisional CID, but HQ weren't interested in explanations . . .

Burrell entered. "Word's through from vehicle identification on the glass in the Yates case. It came from a Vauxhall, made between four and a half and five years ago."

"They can be that exact?"

"Seems so, Guv. The manufacturers of the lamp units were

trying out a new type of glass in the hope that on damp roads at night dazzle would be less; it didn't work out all that well and the glass was more expensive to produce, so it was dropped."

"Are we in luck at last?"

"Six months means a whole lot of Vauxhalls must have been produced."

"Ask Swansea for a list of all Prussian blue shooting brakes registered in the county in the relevant period."

Burrell left. Ten to one, Meyer decided, Burrell had quickly seen reason for deep pessimism. At night, shape could be mistaken; even if it had been a blue Vauxhall shooting brake, it might have been from a distant county; it was three weeks since the accident and the more time that passed, the better chance the driver had of covering his tracks . . .

Eight

L aura made a point of chatting with Mrs Catlin when the latter had her midday cup of tea since modern democracy demanded that if one were to keep one's daily happy, one had to treat her as only a little short of a personal friend. The front door bell rang. "We'd better see who that is."

Mrs Catlin nodded, but made no effort to move.

Laura left the kitchen, made her way up the passage into the hall. When she opened the front door, she faced a man, dressed with little regard for conventional smartness, whom she did not know. "Yes?" she said, making it clear she had no intention of buying an encyclopaedia.

"Detective Constable Parker, local CID. Mrs Ryan?"

"Yes."

"Perhaps you'd be kind enough to say if you still own a blue Astra shooting brake, just over four and a half years old?"

"Why d'you want to know?"

"It's in connection with an on-going investigation."

He obviously expected to be asked inside. Bumptious by nature as well as lacking the slightest sartorial taste. It would have been more suitable to leave him standing on the doorstep, but the morning was raw and she was already beginning to feel cold. "You'd better come inside."

She led the way into the sitting-room. "Well?" she asked, as she sat.

Parker, amused by the thought that she expected him respectfully to remain standing, also sat. "It's like this, Mrs Ryan. Three weeks ago, a woman in Randers Cross was getting out of her car at night when she was hit by another car which did not stop. She died from her injuries."

"I don't understand why that should concern me."

"The hit-and-run car has been identified as a dark blue Astra shooting brake and according to Swansea, your husband owns one."

"And if he does?"

"Then we need to eliminate the possibility that it was his car which was involved in the accident."

"That should be obvious."

"Why so?"

"My good man, he does not go around the countryside hitting people."

Parker would dearly have liked to reply, 'My good lady . . .' but the police were forbidden to give as good as they got. "He has not had an accident in his Astra?"

She ignored the question.

"Is it here so I can examine it?"

"Why d'you want to do that?"

"It's standard procedure when we are eliminating vehicles from our investigations."

"I have already told you, my husband's car has not been involved in an accident."

"Nevertheless, I need to have a quick look at it."

"Are you trying to be impertinent?"

His quick temper finally breached his self-control. "I can assure you that if I were, I'd be far more successful."

Her lips tightened.

"Is the Astra here?"

"No."

"Where is it, then?" He wondered if her bloody-minded manner was not a sign of perceived superiority, but of an uneasy conscience?

"My husband has it because he did not walk to work today."

"Then the car will be parked near his office?"

"No."

"Why's that?"

"He has to drive somewhere to consult with a client who's too ill to leave home."

"When will he be returning from that visit?"

"I've no idea . . . Is that all?"

He stood. "Would you tell your husband I'll be in touch with him some time tomorrow just to wrap everything up. Thank you for your helpful co-operation," he added, managing not to sound sarcastic.

She didn't bother to say goodbye even though she doubted he'd be able to understand the social significance of this omission. It seemed an age since the police had been recruited from the right sort of persons.

The cordless phone was on the piecrust table by her side and she picked it up, extended the aerial, switched it on, dialled.

"Amshot and Feakin," said a woman with a carefully modulated voice.

"It's Mrs Ryan. Is my husband in, Sarah?"

"Actually, I'm Barbara."

She could never be bothered to remember who was who. "Is he there?"

"Would you hold on a moment?"

She waited.

"I'm sorry, Mrs Ryan, but Mr Ryan hasn't returned yet. Mrs Sommerville says she doesn't know when to expect him and if you need to speak to him urgently, she suggests you try his mobile. He may have remembered to switch it on."

"Thank you." She cut the connection. Mrs Sommerville was a young widow, quite good looking in a common way, who'd have lifted her skirt very quickly if encouraged. Typically, the thought had never occurred to Ryan. Laura found that amusing and saw no reason to feel grateful.

She could never remember the number of his mobile. She switched off the cordless, went through to the hall. By the side of the phone was the booklet in which were listed all the frequently used numbers and she checked the one she wanted, dialled it. After several rings, a sepulchral voice informed her that the phone was not switched on and if she wished, she could leave a message. As she replaced the receiver, Mrs Catlin appeared at the head of the stairs. "I've finished your room."

"Then perhaps you can do the main guest suite."

"There ain't much time left."

"Do as much as possible." Even at the distance, she could make out Mrs Catlin's expression of resentment. It was so typical of her to expect to be paid for work she didn't do. Laura returned to the sitting-room, making certain the door was shut to prevent any chance of being overheard, picked up the cordless phone and dialled.

"Leegate Containers," said the middle aged, lumpish woman who was the only other worker in the office.

"It's Mrs Ryan. Is my cousin there?"

"Yes, he is. I'll put you through."

After a very brief pause, Tyler said: "Is something up?"

"That's one hell of a warm greeting!"

"In business hours, it's business greetings. What's the problem?"

Perversely, his roughness which lay just beneath the

smooth surface, had always attracted her. "Maybe I won't tell you."

"So goodbye."

"Hang on, you bastard. You need to know what's been happening."

"I doubt it."

"You sound really grim-eyed."

"Too grim-eyed to waste any more time."

"There's no need to be so rude."

"I'm up to my eyebrows trying to cope with bloody idiots who won't do as they're told."

"And you can't take even a little time off to listen to me?"

"Now you're on my wavelength."

"No time even when I tell you I've had a detective along, asking questions?"

"Have you been keeping a bawdy house?"

"If I were, I wouldn't have the likes of you in it . . . He's trying to identify a car and had the impudence to suggest it could be Alan's."

There was a brief silence, then Tyler, his tone changed, said: "Why was he interested in that lump of inertia?"

"There's been some sort of accident in which a woman was killed and the car drove on. The police are trying to identify it."

"And what in the wide world has made them think it could have been Alan acting in so unchivalrous a manner?"

"The car was a blue shooting brake."

"Did the detective explain how he knew that?"

"No. He was so impertinent, I got rid of him as soon as I could."

"Where did the accident take place?"

"He did say, but I can't remember. Something Cross, I think."

"Presumably, they're questioning everyone who owns a similar car?"

"I suppose so."

"Alan's hasn't been specifically picked out?"

"Why should it have been?"

"No possible reason, but the police never restrict themselves to possibilities ... Did this detective want to see the car?"

"Yes, but Alan's got it today and he isn't at the office. The detective said he's going to get in touch to arrange to examine it. That's even though I kept telling him he was wasting his time."

"Since we pay for their time, they have no objection to wasting it."

"Keith—"

"I'm still on line."

"The accident happened three weeks ago."

"So?"

"That's when you had Alan's car because yours had broken down."

"BMWs do not break down. It simply was not on full song."

"But you did have the Astra then."

"And now you're wondering whether I had that accident?"

"Well—"

"Your sense of loyalty is touching."

"I . . . I don't understand why the police seemed so interested in the car."

"You explained that only a moment ago. What they're doing is routine and doesn't begin to mean anything definite. They're looking for signs of collision, the Astra doesn't have

56

any, end of story. Your mind can be at rest . . . To more pleasant things. Know what talking to you has done?"

"What?"

"Find out by coming to my flat this afternoon."

"My God! that's a bit of a change. When I first spoke to you, you were bloody rude."

"Which makes my conversion all the more estimable. Three o'clock."

"I don't know I can."

"Playing hard to get?"

"It's Alan. I can't be certain when he'll be back and if he'll come here straight away or go to the office first."

"Get Margie to cover for you."

"She says I've been doing that so often, you must be something special."

"Tell her to get in touch with me and I'll teach her I am."

"Like hell!"

"You don't feel charitable towards your best friend?"

"Charity starts and ends at home."

Nine

Parker left the CID Escort and walked towards the side entrance of divisional HO; half-way across, he met Lipman. "I'm just back from having a word with Mrs Ryan. She's a real bitch, if ever I've met one."

"Hardly relevant."

Parker contented himself with a silent "Up yours, mate". "She says their Astra hasn't been involved in any accident."

"But one of the letters is P."

Parker said nothing.

"You examined the car?"

"Her husband's off with it somewhere and she didn't know when he'll be returning. I said we'd be in touch tomorrow."

"Where was the car on the twenty-second of last month?"

"I didn't ask."

"Why not?"

"She was spitting tacks as it was because I dared ask the likes of her any questions. If I'd started getting pointed, I reckon they'd have become six inch nails. Didn't seem to be any point in causing too much hassle unless there seemed to be definite reason and that means examining the car."

"You must have gone the wrong way about questioning her."

"Could be. So why don't you take over the next time and have her eating out of your hand?"

Lipman said nothing, walked on.

Leegate was mentioned in the Etchinham Chronicles and referred to as a town with a thriving port trade. However, in the late thirteenth century, there had been what contemporaries confusingly referred to as 'a swirling of the land' and the river had changed course, rendering the port useless. Without the trade, the town had slowly decayed. Then, in the middle of the nineteenth century, a local landowner had conceived the idea of forming a company whose aim would be to restore prosperity to the town by diverting the river back to its original course and rebuilding the docks. Since his motive had been largely altruistic, the idea had bankrupted both him and the company. However, work had advanced to the point where men who were interested only in their own prosperity formed a second company and saw the work completed at great profit.

Succeeding years had brought cycles of prosperity and hardship to the town until it had been decided to use the port as one of the staging posts for the invasion of Normandy and it had been enlarged and modernised. This time, prosperity persisted. In the eighties, three blocks of luxury flats had been built on the high ground on the western outskirts of the town and Tyler's was the penthouse on the tenth floor of the most westerly; from it there was a panoramic view of the Channel.

Laura sat up on the king size bed. "That was disgusting!"

Tyler laughed.

"It was!"

"Trying to salve your suburban conscience? Variety is the spice of life and you enjoyed every spicy moment."

"But I didn't expect—"

"Always expect the unexpected."

She giggled.

"Share your joy."

"What would Alan say if I suggested trying what we've just done?"

"He'd probably call for a service of exorcism . . . God knows why you married someone so prim and proper."

"You'd left me, hadn't you?"

"Not voluntarily."

"Didn't make any difference; I had to live. When I met him at Margie's and she said he was well off . . . She never added she hardly knew him and he was a friend of a friend. How was I to know he's bloody Victorian?"

"By offering him a sample to find out what he was really like before you said yes at the altar."

"He wouldn't screw until we married."

"You expect me to believe that?"

"It's true."

"The man's a living fossil. You definitely should have waited for me."

"And if I had, I'd spend my time knowing you're after every married woman you meet because of the extra pleasure from making a fool of the husband."

"What a nasty character you seem to think I have." He clasped his hands behind his head as that rested on the pillow. "Shall I make an embarrassing confession? Since being with you again, I've not so much as looked at another woman."

"Like hell you haven't."

"Having sipped nectar, would I sour my tongue with vinegar?"

"You'd stick your tongue anywhere." She looked at her watch. "I must move."

"No second helping?"

"He'll be returning home very soon if he's not already there."

"Margie can tell him that she and you spent the whole afternoon discussing the merits of your husbands." He unclasped his hands. "There's a range of spices you haven't sampled yet."

He watched her climb off the bed and cross to the chair. "Do you realise you folded up all your clothes with the greatest possible care?"

"What if I did?" She picked up a pair of lace edged pants.

"It shows you've been conditioned by your lord and master to act in a well-bred manner even at the most exciting moments."

Pants in one hand, she swung round. "I suppose that's why I'm here? And he's not my lord or master." Then, illogically, she suddenly began to defend her husband. "He's old fashioned, God knows, but that's because of the way he was brought up. His parents were so prim and proper that they probably screwed with their eyes shut."

"Tell me something."

She stepped into the pants, pulled them up. "What?"

"You said that the detective's returning to have a look at his car. He'll be asked where it was the night of the accident. What's he going to answer?"

"How would I know?"

"If he's so old fashioned, he'll tell the the truth."

She continued dressing.

"You don't see that this raises a problem?"

"No."

"He'll explain that I had the car that night which means the police will start questioning me. They'll discover I've been inside. They're obviously not getting anywhere with their inquiries and with all the media attention, they'll have become desperate to make an arrest. The moment they think I could be a possible, they'll land the job on me."

"You're not trying to say that they'll prove you guilty when they know you're not?"

"I'm saying just that."

"The police wouldn't do such a thing."

"It could be your simpleton husband speaking. My dear, sweet naïf, when a crime's been committed and the police can't make an honest arrest, but the pressure's on them, they grab the nearest ex-con and hang the job on him."

"But—"

"So you're going to have to persuade Alan to suffer a little lapse of memory."

"You're not suggesting he lies to the police?"

"No blasphemy. All he need do is forget he lent me his car. Where's the harm?"

"But why? The police will look at it and know it couldn't have had anything to do with the accident."

"I've just explained. The moment they learn I'm an ex-con—"

"Don't tell them."

"They can smell one as quickly as I can smell a split. I'll be in their sights from the beginning. Sure, the car doesn't show any signs of collision because it hasn't been in one, but they'll demand it's taken in for a thorough search and when they don't find anything, they'll plant something – a fibre from the woman's clothing, or anything else that'll work for 'em. Then they'll have me cold."

"You said you went to a business meeting?"

"That's right."

"Then you were with someone who can tell the police you weren't on the road at the time of the accident."

"You know something? You're beginning to sound like a prosecuting mouthpiece."

Her voice became shrill. "You were with a woman."

"It was a business meeting, the plane was endlessly delayed, I was in my hotel bedroom, on my own, watching television. That gives the law the perfect chance to stitch me up."

"D'you swear you weren't with a woman?"

"Didn't I have to rush from your place before we'd had time to make music? Would I—"

"If the plane was so delayed, you didn't have to rush."

"I thought it would be on time, didn't I? The bloody fool who phoned me didn't have the intelligence to find out. What's got you so tight? Would I have cleared off like that to meet a woman who couldn't even begin to understudy you?"

She finished dressing.

"Well, would I?"

"I suppose not." She crossed to the bed and stroked his cheek. "I'm sorry, my darling, but I get so jealous."

"Next time, look in the mirror and see how stupid you're being."

She leaned over and kissed him.

As she straightened up, he said, as if there could be no doubt: "You'll persuade him easily enough."

"I . . . I don't know. He's so starchy about anything to do with the law."

"Employ your feminine wiles. Remember, you fail and I'll be back inside and it'll be for so many years that when I come out I won't be good for anything but a game of draughts."

Ten

Ironically, it was Ryan who yawned as he set the upstairs alarms.

"Was it a very wearisome day?" she asked solicitously.

"More a frustrating one. My client was intent on proving that a fool and his money are very soon parted."

She undid the belt of her dress, reached behind her back to pull down the zip.

"Did you manage to make him see sense?"

"I hope so."

"He'd have to be a complete fool not to have listened to you." She lifted the dress up over her head.

"What kind of a day have you had?"

"Nothing out of the ordinary."

"That's bad luck."

She smiled. She removed her embroidered petticoat. As he yawned again, she said: "Are you too tired?"

"Too tired for what?"

She undid her brassière and let it fall to the ground. "If you ask that, you must be."

It was a long time since it had been she who had initiated sex. He crossed to where she stood and ran his hands down her body. "A man wakes up very smartly when Calypso sings."

*   *   *

She lay on her side, he on his back. She put her right hand on his chest and very gently curled and uncurled several hairs. "Did I mention that a detective called this morning?"

"No. What did he want?"

"Do you remember that an elderly woman was knocked down in Randers Cross three weeks ago and died soon afterwards?"

"Can't say I do."

"It turned out that she'd been awarded the George Medal when she was young."

"Now I'm with it. The car which hit her drove on. It's incredible how callous people have become. *Tempora mutantur et nos mutamur in illis.*"

"Probably!"

"If you can get away with something, never mind who suffers . . . How can that possibly have anything to do with us?"

"The police say the car was a blue Vauxhall shooting brake, four and a half to five years old."

"So now they're checking all cars which fit that description?"

"I told the detective we'd never had any kind of an accident, but he wants to see the car tomorrow; I explained you were away."

"I'm at the office all day so I'll leave it here. He can look at it when that suits you."

"There is a bit of a problem."

"What's that?"

"He wants to have a word with you as well."

"Then it'll be easiest if I drive to the office and after checking my work schedule, phone him to say when's best for him to come there. What's his name?"

"Detective Constable Parker."

"Right."

"The thing is, it's not quite that simple."

"No? I thought I was the one who always found complications?"

Her voice sharpened. "Why can't you be serious?"

"Sorry." His surprise was obvious.

She hastened to move until she could rest her breasts on his chest. "I'm sorry, my love, I didn't mean to bitch. But talking about him gets me annoyed."

"Why so?"

"He was so cockily determined to show he was every bit as good as me."

"You're saying he was rude? I'll have a word with the divisional superintendent whom I've met a few times. A very sensible kind of chap."

"He wasn't actually rude; he didn't say anything definite, it was just his attitude."

"The old sea dog who knows exactly how far he can take things without being put on defaulters. The only practical way of dealing with his kind is completely to ignore his unspoken insolence, leaving him frustrated because he doesn't know whether or not you realise he's been insolent."

She moved, to lie against him. "Have you forgotten something?"

"Probably. Old men forget."

"You're not even middle aged! ... We didn't have the Astra on the night of the accident because Keith had it when he thought his car wasn't behaving properly. So what happens?"

"As regards the detective? I explain and he'll have a word with Keith if he reckons that's necessary."

"Do you have to say that Keith had the car?"

"Of course."

"But since Keith didn't knock the woman down, what can it matter?"

"The police must be told the truth, whether or not that's of any consequence."

"You're beginning to sound all official."

"I know I become pompous where the law's concerned—"

"Not pompous. Just official."

"A fine-edged difference? The thing is, I believe that uncorrupted justice marks the division between civilisation and chaos ... And now, no doubt, you're going to tell me I've become a politician, lauding his patriotism at election time."

"I'm going to tell you that if everyone thought like you, it would be a much nicer world. Only ... I don't know how to say this so you'll be able to understand."

He was surprised – she didn't usually measure her words. He spoke with mild facetiousness. "So long as you keep things simple, I'll probably manage."

"Keith and I are so close because we were brought up together whenever his parents were abroad – but you know that, don't you?"

"You have told me, yes."

"When he started mixing with the wrong crowd, I was terribly worried and tried again and again to persuade him to find other friends. But he just wouldn't listen ... You'll never tell him I've said all this, will you?"

"Not if you don't want me to."

"In the end, he was ..." She paused, then ended in a rush. "He was sent to jail." She gripped his hand.

"On what charge?" he asked quietly.

"Does ... does that matter?"

"Having got this far, it'll be best if you tell me everything."

"You must believe that Keith didn't realise what kind of

people the other two really were; he thought they were just like him, wild but not vicious."

"There was violence?"

"Yes," she whispered.

"In what circumstances?"

"They broke into a warehouse. They'd been told there wasn't a night watchman, but there was and he tried to stop them. The other two . . . they hurt the poor man badly."

When he'd first been told about her cousin, a few years after their marriage, he'd suspected some kind of skeleton in the family cupboard; there had been confirmation of a kind when she'd been so angry at his suggesting this and promising her that nothing could affect their relationship. He'd been hurt by her reaction, even more by the fact that she had not confided in him initially. "It must have been a very sad and bitter time."

She squeezed his hand. "When I visited him in jail, it was so awful it was like someone was screaming in my head."

"Was he still in jail when we married?"

"Yes."

"So you didn't visit him thereafter?"

"I . . . I did when I could without you knowing."

"Why the hell didn't you tell me and you could have seen him whenever that was possible?"

"I was ashamed; and afraid."

"Afraid of what?"

"That you'd be so contemptuous of me for having a cousin in jail that you'd throw me out."

"How could you even imagine I'd do such a thing?"

"Soon after we first met, you told me how much you hated criminals because they threatened society."

"I couldn't have contempt for you if you had a dozen

relatives in jail. Especially as you did everything in your power to stop him going to the bad."

"You're so wonderfully understanding." She kissed him.

"No more secrets between us?"

"Never, ever . . . You do now understand why you musn't tell the police that Keith had the car, don't you?"

"Not really. The fact that he's been convicted in the past is irrelevant."

"He says the police would know he's been to jail and so if they can't find the real driver, they'll fake the evidence to prove it was him."

"They don't do that sort of thing."

"I knew you'd say that. But it does happen. Look at the cases there've been when the police have been shown to have altered the evidence."

"I'm afraid that has happened," he said regretfully. "The trouble comes when they are convinced someone is guilty, but can't get sufficient strong evidence to prove that in court."

"The papers have gone on about the woman's death and calling on the police to find the driver. They're going to do anything to look successful."

"This is really all hypothetical. When the police look at our car and see it can't have suffered any damage, that'll be an end of things."

"Not if they plant something in the car like a thread from the woman's coat."

"Good God! that's drawing a hell of a long bow."

"But it could happen. You've just admitted that it has."

"When the police were convinced they were dealing with the guilty person."

"How can you be so certain? Maybe they just wanted an arrest and looked around for someone they could use."

"They wouldn't try to frame someone they had every reason to believe to be innocent."

"You hope that's true. You don't know it is . . . You've got to understand. When Keith came out of prison, he could have really gone to the bad. But I made him promise he'd break free from the past. He's always been clever and sharp and when he found the job he's with now, he made a wonderful success of things, as you know. But if the firm learns he's been in jail, they'll throw him out."

"They can't without good cause; I doubt that in the circumstances of his evident success a previous conviction would be held to be that unless he'd made a specific denial of any criminal record when engaged."

"Perhaps they'd make him redundant. The redundancy money wouldn't be all that much and he would be terribly bitter. I know him almost as well as I know myself. He's done wonderfully well and is proud of himself. Being thrown out would knock him sideways, destroy all his pride, turn him back on to his old ways and friends. It would mean total disaster for him . . . Alan, sweet, it would break my heart to see him back in trouble. Please, please, don't let that happen; please do as I ask."

His instinct was to say that whatever the circumstances, honesty had to be the best policy. But he could appreciate that not only would he sound unctuously sanctimonious, there were times when that hoary cliché was, in practical terms, wrong. This could be one such time . . .

"I've been through it all once. I don't think I could go through it again."

"You'll have to let me think about it."

Later, when she was asleep, he tried to find justification for the decision he knew he was going to make because he could not bear the thought of her being emotionally savaged. Justice

demanded truth, yet a lie did not necessarily deny justice.
There was no justice when an innocent man was put in peril,
therefore it had to be right to do whatever was necessary to
prevent that happening. When evidence was irrelevant, there
could be no practical harm in withholding it . . .

Eleven

The internal phone buzzed. Sarah, a great believer in chris-tian names, said: "Alan, there's a Detective Constable Parker wants to see you."

"Send him along," Ryan replied.

Parker entered the room. " 'Morning, Mr Ryan."

"Good morning. Do you want to go down and look at my car?"

"We can have a word or two first." Parker sat.

Even after so brief a meeting, Ryan understood why Laura had been so annoyed. Clearly, Parker had an amusedly contemptuous regard for the older social mores – a touch of the Australian. "How can I help you?"

"It goes like this. We've reason to believe the car involved in the accident to Mrs Yates was a blue Vauxhall shooting brake, between four and a half and five years old. So we're looking at all such vehicles to see if any of 'em bear signs of contact. I'm sure, with you being a solicitor, I don't need to explain that wanting to check your car doesn't mean there's any hint of suspicion. And the same goes for me asking you now if you'll say where you were on the evening of the twenty-second of last month, which was a Tuesday"

Absurdly, Ryan remembered the day at school when the headmaster had asked him if he knew anything about the broken window in the games pavilion; to protect a friend, he'd denied that he did, terrified the lie would immediately be exposed. It had not been and that had taught him that authority was not omniscient. "I don't remember going anywhere or doing anything special, which means we were at home." The more willing he appeared to be to help, the less likely that what he said would be questioned; small details, if carefully presented, could add corroboration far beyond their punching weight. "But to make absolutely certain, I'll phone my wife who acts as unpaid social secretary." He smiled with self mockery. "She'll look in her diary . . . Excuse me a moment." He lifted the receiver of the outside phone, dialled. Mrs Catlin answered the call with a curt "Yes", despite all the times she had been asked to be more politely welcoming.

When Laura was on the other end of the line, he said: "Detective Constable Parker's here and he's asked if I can say where I was on the evening of the twenty-second of last month. I've told him that as far as I know, we were both at home, but you might look in your appointments diary to see if we were out anywhere."

"What appointments diary?"

"That's right. The twenty-second; a Tuesday."

"Are you all right?"

"Of course."

"Is it . . . is it going badly?"

"Far from it. I see. Sorry to have troubled you, but I did want to be certain." He replaced the receiver, looked across the desk. "We had no engagement that night so we were definitely at home."

"Thanks for taking the trouble." Parker stood. "Now, if I can have a quick look at your car and then I'll get out of your hair."

Ryan led the way down the corridor, the flight of stairs, across the reception area – Sarah watched them with open curiosity – along another corridor, and out through the back door to the small, private parking area. "Over there." He pointed.

Parker crossed to the Astra and examined the near-side headlamp. He slowly walked around the car, having to squeeze his way through on the left-hand side because the next car was parked so closely. He came to a stop in front of the bonnet. "It's in pretty good nick for a car this old."

"I keep a dehumidifier in the garage and that's on much of the time in the winter."

"Certainly does the job. My car's half the age and looks as if I've been driving through gorse bushes . . . Well, that's it. Thanks for all your help."

"Glad to do whatever I can."

Ryan returned into the building and went up to his office. As he sat, Mrs Sommerville looked into the room. "Mrs Ryan's twice been on the phone. She seems rather concerned."

"I'll give her a ring." As she shut the door behind herself, he dialled his home number. Laura answered after the second ring. "I know I probably sounded odd when I phoned you just now, but I wanted the detective to think you kept an appointments book because if it didn't list anything for that evening, it meant we didn't go out. It added weight to what I told him."

"Did he believe you?"

"He'd no reason not to."

"Can't you ever answer straightforwardly?"

"He believed me." It was not a time for legal caution.

"You're sure?"

"Positive."

"Thank God."

When he replaced the receiver, he thought that love was almost as dangerously powerful an emotion as poets

75

would have it – it could make a man wilfully betray himself.

When visually examining the Astra, Parker had noted on the tailgate a worn sticker naming Roland Garage – probably put there when the car was sold. He drove on to the forecourt of the garage and parked beyond the petrol pumps, walked into the office. A young woman, black hair drawn tightly back in severe style, looked up from the computer at which she was working.

"Local CID."

"Not again?"

"It's lucky we're so cuddly, isn't it?"

She smiled and this brought warmth and humour to a face that in repose was austerely featured.

"Is Mr Alan Ryan one of your regulars?"

"I can't say off-hand, but the name rings a bit of a bell."

"Check it out, will you, and see if any work's been done on his Astra in the past month."

She fiddled with the edge of the keyboard. "I maybe ought to ask Mr Burchell if it's all right to give you the details."

"If it'll make you happy, have a word with him."

"He's out."

"Then ... Straight, it can't do any harm to anyone telling me."

"Then why are you asking?"

He chuckled. "That's sharp! . . . It's like this. I had to ask Mr Ryan some questions, like I've had to ask them to a lot of other people. He's answered and I'm happy, but the way we work is that everything has to be double-checked even when anyone with half a brain can see it'll be a waste of time. All I'm asking you to do is to confirm that he's not brought the car in for repairs in the past month."

"If you put it like that, I suppose it's all right." She tapped out instructions on the keyboard, studied the VDU, scrolled the list until she had what she wanted. "He is a regular. His car had a service five weeks ago and before that there was a clutch problem in July."

"No repairs to the lights?"

"Like I've just said."

He thanked her, left. At divisional HQ, neither Meyer nor Lipman was in, so he put a brief note on Lipman's desk. That done, he decided that in the absence of authority, there was little reason why he should not go down to the canteen for a coffee.

Parker and Stevens were looking through a recently confiscated catalogue of pornographic videos for sale when Lipman stepped just inside the general room. "This place looks like a junk shop." He pointed. "What's that stuff doing up here?"

"I was just about to take it down, sarge," Stevens said.

"With you lot, it's always just about . . . Bert, the old man wants you. Now, not just about." He left.

"He gets sharper by the day," Stevens said.

"Suffering from promotionitis."

"D'you reckon he'll make DI soon?"

"Only if there's no justice left in the world." Parker closed the catalogue. "If you're paying, let's try forty-one and see if they're as athletic as the description says."

"How about going halves?"

"You want me to pay for looking at something I enjoy free?"

"If you're enjoying what they're supposed to be doing, you're a dirty old man."

"Where's the point to living if you aren't?"

Parker left the general room and walked along the corridor

to the DI's room, knocked on the partially opened door, went in. "You want me, Guv.?"

"I gather you've had a word with Smart and Ryan?" Meyer said, from behind his desk.

"That's right. It's a case of Smart by name, not by nature."

Unlike Lipman, Meyer was more often amused than irritated by Parker's manner and in consequence had a greater appreciation of the DC's talents.

"It took me half an hour to convince him I wasn't about to clap him in irons. In the end, he told me he was with friends and they corroborate him."

"And Ryan?"

Parker spoke slowly. "I don't quite know how to answer."

"Intelligently would be a start."

"He was real helpful. Fair enough, seeing he's a solicitor and they're supposed to be law-abiding when they're not swindling their clients. But he did seem to be trying a shade too hard. Does that make sense?"

"Up to a point. Was there any hesitation in answering any of your questions?"

"Just the reverse."

"You're saying he could be interesting?"

"I can't be certain and that's straight. But when someone makes such a point of being the good citizen . . . Against that, when he said he and his wife were home all that evening, I'd bet a quid to a penny he was telling the truth. It's a bloody conundrum."

"What about his car?"

"No signs of damage and the garage he goes to confirms that no repairs have been done to it in the past month."

"Despite any doubts, doesn't the car say he has to be in the clear?"

"I'm not so certain."

"You seem to have had an uncertain morning." Parker smiled briefly. "Like we knew, it's got a P in its number."

"But not a six. And Mrs Green is the first to admit her eyesight's not all that good."

"It's like this, Guv. His car is over four and a half years old, but you'd think it had just come out of the showroom. My car's half that age and the paintwork says it's been around."

"You're suggesting a respray?"

"If there has been one, I reckon it was a total."

"And every paintshop has been questioned. Could it have been a DIY job?"

"Not unless Ryan has professional gear and is up to professional standards. And I'd say the chances of that are nil."

"Did you comment to him on how his car looked?"

"He said it was so good because he keeps a dehumidifier in the garage."

"Supposedly, that does keep a car in top condition."

"But who's ever owned a car for four and a half years without its being bumped or scraped by some berk?"

"In practical terms, it all adds up to next to nothing. And since he's a solicitor, he's not the man to tangle with unnecessarily."

"Since he's being so co-operative, if we asked to have his car in just to confirm everything's smooth, wouldn't he agree without any hassle?"

"Just as likely to decide enough's enough. His kind have boundaries and if you try to push through 'em, there's trouble."

"But surely it would be worth trying?"

Meyer considered the situation. People could be so old fashioned in outlook that even in an age of self, they did help authority; Ryan might be such a fusser that he had succeeded, against the odds, in keeping his car unscathed; his position in society suggested he was unlikely ever knowingly to break the law. Yet if there were even the sliver of a chance of identifying the driver of the car who had smashed into Mrs Yates and then fled . . . "Go ahead. But if he starts shouting, the whole idea is yours."

"That's not very sporting."

"It's called, protecting your own arse."

Twelve

R yan returned home on Monday evening to find Laura in the large, extensively equipped kitchen. He kissed her. "You're looking very à la mode!"

"In this apron?"

"I was referring to the flour on your face which makes you look as if you're about to step out on the catwalk."

"I've been making pastry." She brushed her cheeks with her hand.

"Are you finished?"

"Why?"

"If you are, we can enjoy a drink."

They left the kitchen and went through to the sitting-room. He crossed to the cocktail cabinet. "What would you like?"

"A brandy and ginger. And now you can tell me why you're in such a good mood?"

He opened the right-hand cabinet door and moved bottles around. "Old Reggie Eccles died recently."

"Who was he?"

"A bit of a fruit cake," he answered as he began to pour.

"Oh, my God! You just couldn't resist that, could you?"

"I'm afraid I've been saving it all day ... He owned Cheetsley Manor."

"Is that the big place on the outskirts of Deeringstone?"

"It is. Experts call it one of the best examples of an

H-shaped stone Elizabethan house in the country. And in addition, there's a three thousand acre estate. Eccles always employed a London law firm, but the heirs have asked us to handle the legal side of things. Quite a feather in our cap!" He carried two glasses across, handed one to her, sat. "Hence my good mood."

"Will it mean a lot of extra money?"

"It will certainly brighten the books."

"Then . . . Pat phoned this morning to say she and Robert are booking on a luxury cruise to the West Indies. Let's join them."

"Hang on. We're not suddenly in Rothschild territory."

"I bet we could easily afford to go, and choose a better cabin than they have, but you just won't because you're worried about the kind of people we'd meet. You should have been a monk."

"I'd have broken my vows on meeting you."

"If you had been one, you wouldn't have met me. And even if you had, you'd have avoided temptation by carefully not looking at me."

"When you were wearing a skirt that ended almost as soon as it began?"

"It wasn't that short."

"I was very tempted to drop a five pound note in order to pick it up."

"Don't be ridiculous. You wouldn't have done anything of the sort because no gentleman ever would."

"You obviously don't know many gentlemen."

She drank. "Before I forget, Caroline and Tommy have invited us to dinner on the fifth of December."

"That's a hell of a long way ahead."

"It's their tenth wedding anniversary and Cary wants to make certain people are free to go to it."

"What is the tenth – silk?"

"Tin."

"That means we need only give a tinny present."

"That's terrible."

"I suppose it is," he agreed.

Ryan was not nearly so conventionally buttoned-up as Laura accused him of being and there were times when he enjoyed the pleasure of excess. He decided to finish the bottle of Marqués de Riscal even though he was aware that there was already a slight blurring to life's edges. He refilled his glass. "By the way, the police want my car for the best part of a day."

"What d'you mean?" she asked sharply.

He cut a piece off the wedge of Cheddar on the cheese dish. "The detective was surprisingly frank – maybe because I'm a lawyer – and admitted that the police aren't really making any progress in their investigation, so now they're asking every owner of a blue Vauxhall shooting brake of the right age to let them have a much closer look at it." He ate the cheese with his fingers – a departure from his normal table manners.

"I hope you told them to go to hell?"

"Of course not. They'll collect the car and bring it back when they've finished and if I like to put in a claim for petrol, it will – to use their very words – be regarded sympathetically." He drank, enjoying the relatively light, dry wine.

"Why? Why didn't you?"

He looked at her and wondered if the curl on her forehead was there by chance or design?

"Can't you answer?" she snapped.

He told himself to concentrate. "There just didn't seem any good reason to argue."

83

"You'd fall over backwards to do whatever they wanted."

"I'll help where I can."

"Like a good citizen?"

"Where's the harm?"

"You're so blind that you can't see that if they want to look at your car again it's because they think you could be a liar?"

"That's possible. Their training teaches them that even an archangel isn't to be trusted."

"You haven't the self-respect to feel humiliated?"

"I can't see why my co-operating should cause you such concern."

"Maybe you would if you'd drunk less."

"I can still say floccinauc . . . Well, maybe I can't go all the way, but five out of ten for trying."

She stood, crossed to the doorway and left.

He emptied the bottle into his glass. *In vino cave quid dicis quando, et cui.* She was angry because she felt that the police's request was an insult and he didn't feel insulted; he believed it to be his duty to give the police what help he could; he'd drunk too much to say floccinauc . . . how the hell did the rest of the word run?

On Wednesday morning, Parker reported to Meyer. "I've dropped Norman at Ryan's place and he's driving their vehicle to country HQ."

Meyer scratched the lobe of his right ear. "No problems?"

"Only Mrs Ryan bellyaching because we were ten minutes later than we said. Messed up the whole of her social day."

"No doubt she'll overcome that disaster."

"She's a real bitch, but a great bit of crackling with it. I wouldn't mind doing a bit of carving on her joints."

"I'm sure she'd be fascinated to know that," Meyer said dryly.

"It's Laura Ryan, Franchine. How are you?"

"Very well, thank you, Mrs Ryan."

"That's good. There are so many awful colds around at the moment." Laura had begun to make a point of being friendly towards the other woman; one never knew what someone in her position might learn or surmise. "Tell me, is Keith there?"

"I'm afraid he's out at the moment. Should I ask him to phone you when he returns? He won't be long."

"Would you be kind enough? I'm sorry to bother you."

"It's no bother at all."

Laura said goodbye and rang off. She went upstairs and along to the end bedroom where Mrs Catlin was dusting. "When you've finished in here, I'd like you to do the breakfast-room."

"If there's time."

It was always the same story, Laura thought angrily. But the shortage of dailies meant one had to put up with the third rate. She returned downstairs and went into the kitchen where she began to prepare the meal. She liked cooking, a fact which surprised her when she thought about it.

The extension phone on the wall rang. She wiped her hands on a square of kitchen roll, lifted the receiver.

"You want a word?" Tyler said.

"Hang on a minute." She crossed to the door to the passage and made certain it was shut, returned to the phone. "The police were here earlier for the car."

"How d'you mean?"

"They drove the Astra off so they could examine it somewhere."

He said with sharp anger: "You stood there and let 'em?"

"How was I supposed to stop them?"

"By telling 'em to bugger off."

"Alan said they could do it."

"I told you, persuade him to play things our way."

"He's so difficult. He keeps saying it's his duty to help them."

"And you're so useless you haven't changed his mind for him?"

"I've done everything I could."

"Which obviously hasn't been enough. Where are they taking the car?"

"I don't know."

"To the local cop-shop or the vehicle examination centre in Chetsford?"

"I've just said, I don't know."

"You could fill a telephone directory with what you don't know."

"You're not being fair."

"Christ, now you're even talking like your sainted husband. Do you think anything in life is fair?"

"Keith—"

"What?"

"I just wondered . . . it wasn't you in that accident, was it?"

"D'you want a sworn statement?"

"Then surely it doesn't matter about the car? I mean, they can look at it as much as they like."

There was a long pause. "I guess you're right," he finally said, speaking calmly. "They can't find a thing. It's just that the way the coppers act like gauleiters gets me on the raw."

"Are you sorry you've been so nasty to me?"

"No. It keeps you guessing."

"What sort of a bastard are you really?"

"Come along in a couple of hours' time and find out."

Thirteen

Meyer brought a small piece of paper out of his wallet and checked what was written on it. Thankfully, he discovered that Susan's birthday was on the twenty-third, not the thirteenth. The previous year he'd forgotten until the evening when his son had inadvertently reminded him; she had assured him that after many years of happy marriage it really didn't matter, but for once he'd not believed her. She was too emotional not to have been hurt. He wrote 23 in large figures on a sheet of paper and wedged this on the mantelpiece, then ringed 22 on the desk calendar to remind him to buy a present.

The phone rang.

"Vehicles here. Regarding the Astra shooting brake. There are no meaningful traces. But we can say that a recent respray is probable."

"Not certain?"

"For your ears, it's certain; in a court, it's probable."

"How recent?"

"Impossible to be precise; even a guess calls for knowing under what conditions the car's been kept."

"In a garage with a dehumidifier on most of the winter."

"Then we're probably talking about weeks rather than months."

"Was the job done by a professional?"

"No shadow of doubt on that score."

"How could you prove a respray?"

"We'd have to remove a flake of paint right down to bare metal and get NACVI to check the layers of primer, undercoat, and top coat, against makers' specifications for that particular production batch."

"What about the nearside headlight?"

"Can't go beyond saying it's undamaged without removing the unit and checking makers' marks with NACVI and if these don't tell enough of the story, having the glass analysed and compared."

"OK. Do all that."

"What exactly?"

"Remove as big a piece of paint as you need, take out a headlight unit, smashing the glass if the marks aren't good enough."

"Send us a signed agreement from the owner and we'll oblige.".

"At this point, I don't want him to know what's going on."

"Then you've made a bad joke. The paint we might just manage by touching up afterwards. But smashing the headlight would mean having to supply a new unit and without the proper authorisation, we couldn't do that."

"I'll authorise it."

"You're not high enough up the ladder. We need a superintendent's signature on this one."

"Then I'll have to tackle my DCS."

"You can try. But finances have become so tight in our department that we're having to justify to the bloody accountants even the smallest expenditure and this one would be an iffy exercise."

At the conclusion of the call, Meyer used the internal

telephone to tell Lipman he wanted all known ringers in the county questioned over the respraying of an Astra shooting brake. He then called county HQ. As he waited to speak to the detective chief superintendent, he drummed on the desk with the fingers of his right hand. Potter was more politician than field worker, concerned with image rather than result . . .

"Yes?"

"Meyer, E division, sir. I've just received information in the Yates case and I'd be grateful for an opinion."

"Yates? The woman who won the GM years ago and was recently run down and killed in Randers Cross?"

"That's right. There's been very considerable media interest and that's added to the pressure to identify the driver, but as you'll have read in my reports, there's precious little hard evidence. However, some information now in from Vehicles might cheer things up. It does bring a problem, though."

"Which is?"

Meyer explained.

"You're asking me to condone deliberate damage to a civilian's car?"

"No, sir. Asking you whether you will agree that with the media pressure there is on us, it would be reasonable to ask Vehicles to carry out a second and more comprehensive search, accepting that there must be the risk of inadvertently damaging the vehicle, resulting in expense."

"Only if I have a signed statement from you that this second search is essential to the investigation and every possible care will be taken to prevent damage to the car; that should damage unfortunately occur, I have a further signed statement from you making it absolutely clear that the damage was purely accidental."

"You'll have both, sir."

As he rang off, Meyer decided that any and every politician was vulnerable because he was always willing to succeed at someone else's expense.

He rang Vehicles and spoke to the same civilian employee as before. "Can you lay your hands on a headlight unit quickly?"

"Shouldn't be any problem with the main county distributors three roads away."

"Then go. And afterwards, all you need do is sign a statement to the effect that the headlamp was broken accidentally, likewise the damage to the paintwork if that's at all visible after you've touched up."

"And if I find all that difficult because I've a conscience?"

"We'll discuss the peculiarity over a couple of beers next time I'm in Chetsford."

Burrell parked the Astra in front of the smaller gateway of Ragstone Hall. He left the car, crossed the pavement, opened the heavy metal door and went through and into the garden. Having rung the front door bell, he stared out at the lawns, the flower beds, the fountain whose single jet of water was occasionally being flicked by the fitful wind, and the belt of trees. If he'd owned such a property, Helen might never have left him . . .

The door opened. He turned and said: "Detective Constable Burrell, sir. I've brought your car back."

"In one piece?" Ryan asked lightly.

"Of course," he answered very seriously.

"And you're finally satisfied?"

"About what?"

"That it cannot have been involved in the fatal hit-and-run accident?"

"That's for Vehicles to say."

92

"And they haven't said to you?"

"No, sir."

"No doubt I'll hear sooner or later. May I offer you a drink?"

"Not for me, thanks all the same."

"How are you going to get back to the police station?"

"I'm finished for the day now and since I don't live all that far from here, I'm walking." He said goodbye and left. He bitterly wondered why a few had all the good luck and the many, all the bad?

It was drizzling and the forecast had spoken of heavy rain later in the day, so Ryan had driven to the office. Ten minutes after he'd left, Laura phoned Tyler. "The police brought the car back last evening."

"Did they say anything?"

"Not according to Alan."

"Which means they didn't. So you can stop wondering whether I've been lying to you."

"I haven't been," she protested.

"Try to sound more convincing."

"Stop being such a bastard."

"And forego some of my charm?"

"You're the most conceited man I've ever met."

"With every cause."

Fourteen

The rain, at times falling at an angle because of the wind, followed Meyer as he left county HQ. Conscientious, sometimes to a fault, he resented having had to waste two hours at a conference which had covered little ground thanks to two senior officers who were short on ideas, but long on words. His temper was not improved when he found that the only person in CID at divisional HQ was Stevens, who could not tell him what he wanted to know. It was almost one o'clock when Lipman came into his room. "Joe says you're asking about the Yates case?"

"And not getting any bloody answers. We had word of a new ringer who's moved into our patch. Has he been identified?"

"Name of Lister, down from the north – no one knows why – and he's been operating for the past six, seven months. Reputation puts him up high."

"Has he been questioned?"

"Not yet."

"Why not?"

"Bert was down for the job, but then we had a very urgent request from county which had to be dealt with so I put him on that."

"I thought I said the ringer was to be questioned just as soon as he could be given a name?"

Lipman said nothing.

"When I give an order, I expect it to be carried out."

"As the request came from county, I judged it to have priority."

"In this division, I name the priorities. I want Lister questioned right away and I want answers."

"From all accounts, he's a difficult customer."

"Pressure him until he's pliable."

"He's an old hand at the game."

"A woman was killed by a drunken driver almost a month ago and we still haven't landed him yet. So stop finding excuses before they're needed."

"Yes, sir." Lipman left.

Meyer silently swore. Because of a sense of frustration, he'd allowed Lipman's smooth, cocksure attitude to annoy him to the point where he'd become irrational. A request from county HQ was in truth a command, clearly taking precedence over a long running case in which little progress was being made; a detective inspector who called for pressure to be put on a witness was in danger of being accused of advocating illegal methods of interrogation.

Lipman answered the phone call from Vehicles on the Wednesday morning.

"NACVI have reported in the Yates case. Analysis proves the paint cannot be original so there definitely has been a respray. As regards the headlight glass which was so unfortunately broken . . ." The speaker laughed. "The unit is not original, but a replacement manufactured just two years ago."

"Anything more?"

"What more do you want? Confirmation that the wheels are round?"

After the call was over, Lipman stared at the top of his desk, his gaze unfocused. He accepted that Meyer was good at his job, but there were times when he inadvisably became too involved in a case. Since scores of people were killed on the roads every week, it was irrational to become concerned about any one victim. Yet there was an indication that he had become so in this case. During the phone call just ended, the other man had laughed and the inference had been unmistakable – the glass of the headlamp had been deliberately broken so that it could be analysed. That sort of action could lead to big trouble. And when a DI landed in the mud, his detective sergeant was very liable to be splashed. It was time to work out how to remain at a safe distance . . .

Ryan was talking to a client when the internal phone buzzed. He picked up the receiver. "Well?" he said, not trying to hide his irritation.

"I thought you should know that Detective Inspector Meyer and Detective Constable Parker are here," Mrs Sommerville said. "They say they must speak to you."

"I'm in conference."

"I have told them that."

"They'll have to wait." He replaced the receiver. "Sorry about that," he said to the client, an elderly, wealthy, over-dressed and overbearing woman of contentious nature and therefore of profitable concern to Amshot and Feakin. As she began to detail once again the incompetence of the firm which had refurbished three of the rooms in her house, he tried to assess why two detectives, one of them senior, wished to speak to him when there was every reason to believe the police had accepted his car could not have been involved in the fatal accident?

When she left, he escorted her down to the outside door.

97

The partners proffered an old fashioned courtesy even to harridans. The two detectives, who'd been leafing through the magazines on the table in the waiting area, came forward and Meyer introduced himself.

Once in his room, Ryan placed a second chair in front of the desk, then sat. "I hope this won't take long. I do have rather a busy day."

Meyer said: "We'll be as quick as possible. There are a few facts we need to check."

"You still haven't identified the car?"

"I'm afraid not."

"But you surely accept that it could not have been mine?"

"Not exactly."

"Why not?"

"I imagine that will become clear. Mr Ryan, as you know, your car has been examined by experts. They say it has recently been resprayed. Do you agree?"

"I answered that in the negative some time ago."

"Perhaps you'd answer it again."

"It has not been resprayed recently, or at any other time in the past."

"You bought it new. So if it has been resprayed, this must have happened during your ownership."

"The key word is 'if'."

"Tests show that the composition of the paint now covering the body is different from the composition of the paint used at the factory at the time your car was produced."

"Then either the tests were incorrectly carried out or the factory records are wrong."

"Neither is likely. Again, the nearside lamp unit was not fitted at the factory."

"What are your grounds for claiming that?"

"I can't answer you since I am not a technician."

"I think, Inspector, that on the contrary, you could very well tell me. Just as you can explain how it was possible for an analysis of the paint of my car to be made."

Meyer said nothing.

"Leaving aside for the moment the question of wrongfully obtained evidence – about which a High Court judge has recently had several scathing comments to make – what is the point to all you've said?"

"We are convinced your Astra has recently suffered damage necessitating a respray and a new headlamp unit. We're inviting you to explain how such damage was caused."

"My car has not been involved in an incident which has resulted in damage to it."

"Then why have you had it resprayed?"

"I have repeatedly told you, I have not."

"Evidence proves you wrong."

"Accepting the evidence – which I do not – then the only possibility is that the respray occurred before I bought the car."

"Why should that have happened?"

"You would need to speak to the manufacturers and the distributors to find the answer. I can only make the suggestion that when there is over-production by the factories, many cars are left in fields until they can be sold on; inevitably, there's corrosion. Presumably, some cars become so marked that they have to be resprayed."

"Had that happened, the details would have been noted by the National Centre For Vehicle Identification. In any case, the respraying is recent, probably very recent."

"Impossible."

"You can't offer a more helpful answer?"

"I see no reason to do so."

"Since you are a solicitor, I'd have thought that the inference raised by the evidence is so clear that you'd have been very quick to explain."

"You are asserting, therefore it is up to you to substantiate your assertions. Since I know they cannot be substantiated, I see no need to explain."

"The nearside lamp pod of your car is not original."

"As I have never had it replaced, it must be."

"When the car was produced, a new type of glass was being used in all the headlamps. As the headlamp in your car does not carry that glass, it cannot be original. In fact, the unit was made within the past two years."

"Once again, impossible."

"Are you suggesting someone would have replaced the unit without any reference to you?"

"I am saying that I do not accept your hypothesis; however, if, in fact, it is correct, I have no idea how or why the replacement occurred."

"I will suggest why. You were out in your car on the night of the twenty-second of October. You probably had dinner with friends and drank too much and when you left to return home, you were under the influence. You rounded the corner into Aspinall Road far too quickly, lost control, and slammed into Mrs Yates who had just got out of her car. You were sufficiently with it to realise that if you stopped, you'd be breathalysed and inevitably be charged with a very serious motoring offence; if that happened, you would almost certainly be jailed and struck off The Rolls. Banking on the fact – well known to you through your work – that when the shockingly unexpected happens, few people are able to take any immediate relevant action or even to gather a coherent impression of events, you decided to drive on, convinced no one would have noted the registration number of your car.

Later, you found the near-side headlamp had been smashed in the collision and there was very slight damage to the bodywork. Again due to your knowledge of how the law works, you realised that the police would check with garages and repair shops to learn if they had been called on to carry out repairs consistent with the damage likely to have been caused in the crash. So you found someone willing, at a price, secretly to make the repairs and respray the whole car because a patching job would have given the game away."

"Ingenious, Inspector, but a theory suffering from one fatal disadvantage."

"Which is?"

"It's totally incorrect."

"When a car fits the known characteristics of the vehicle involved . . ."

"As I have previous explained, I was at home all that evening. My wife has confirmed the fact."

"As was remarked in a past case, 'She would say that, wouldn't she?'"

"You are calling her a liar?"

"I should prefer to say that she has a very strong sense of loyalty."

"You suggest I was at dinner with friends. Can you name them? Have you questioned them? Do they agree I was at dinner with them and drank too much?"

"No."

"Hardly surprising, since none of our friends live near Randers Cross. Have you identified the man who supposedly did all this work on my car?"

"No."

"It would seem that it is not imagination you lack, but any vestige of proof that this has the slightest connection with fact."

"We've proof your car was involved in the fatal accident."

"Proof? You claim it has neither the paintwork nor a headlamp it would be expected to have; if so, that is anomalous, not proof of involvement in the accident. That is impossible. At the time, I was at home."

"Juries draw logical conclusions. If a man owns a car which was involved in a fatal accident and he fails to offer any realistic evidence to the contrary, they will assume that he was driving it." Meyer stood. "We'll be seeing you again, no doubt." He left, followed by Parker who, uncharacteristically, had remained silent.

Ryan stared at the closed door for a long time.

Fifteen

When Ryan returned home, Laura was in an exuberant mood; he did not miss the irony of this. She pressed against him as she kissed him. "There," she said, as she stepped back, "how's that for a welcome home? Uplifting?"

"Great."

"You could try to sound as if you meant it!"

"I've had a very heavy day." He hung his mackintosh on the coat-stand.

"The troubles of the world are on your shoulders? What's it this time? That silly little man with halitosis who will get too close when he talks to you? ... Come and see what I found in the new shop which has just opened up in High Street."

He followed her into the sitting-room and was not surprised to see on the settee a large cardboard box, from under the lid of which there projected a corner of white tissue paper.

She went over to the settee, but did not immediately open the box. "You're not to become even more grumpy and lecture me about saving for old age."

"Presumably, I need to brace myself?"

She lifted the lid and brought out a lime green dress. "The moment I saw it, it was me." She held it in front of herself. "Don't you think it's just perfect?"

"What there is of it."

"You're such a prude."

"Only where my own wife's concerned, not other people's."

"Typical male attitude! Shall I wear it when we're having dinner with Anne and Robert. I'll tell her it's an original Galliano. She's so gormless she won't know it isn't and will be as jealous as hell."

"A recipe for a cheerful party."

"My God, you really are a glum this evening! And there was I feeling life was bubbles. You don't like seeing other people happy, do you?"

"That's ridiculous."

"It's fact."

"I'm sorry, but I really have had one hell of a day."

As she carefully folded the frock and replaced it in the box, he went over to the cocktail cabinet. "What would you like to drink?"

"Something sweet would make a welcome change. Give me a Cinzano and soda."

He poured the drinks, handed her a glass, stood with his back to the fireplace.

"Do you have to look so pompous?" she demanded.

"I had another visit from the police. This time it was a detective inspector and a detective constable."

Her change of manner was immediate. "What did they want?"

"They're claiming my car's recently had a total repaint and the nearside headlight has been replaced."

"You haven't had anything done to it."

"As I told them. But they insist forensic tests prove their assertions."

"Why are they being so stupid?"

"When Mrs Yates was hit by the car, the car suffered damage. Consequently, the police carried out the usual

104

procedures and contacted all garages and suppliers to ask
for details that would give them a lead on the car. But if
the driver of the car was smart, he'd have realised this and
taken steps to have the repairs carried out in secrecy. In turn,
the police have been on the lookout for possible cars which
have recently been repaired."

"If yours had had that done to it, they'd now suspect it
was the one in the accident?"

"Yes."

"Haven't you told them how ridiculous that would
be?"

"Of course. Their answer is that they prefer the forensic
evidence to my evidence."

"You're not saying they really do think it could be your
car which hit the woman?"

"They're clearly convinced that it was."

"But that's just impossible."

He drank, put the glass down on the mantelpiece. "As far
as I can tell, the forensic evidence has to be wrong. Proving
that it is would be difficult, but not impossible; the average
scientist's claim of divine veracity can usually be challenged.
But for the moment, I'm going to assume that what the police
are claiming is true."

"Why, when you know it can't be?"

"Because I do not know it can't be."

"For God's sake, what are you suggesting now?"

"Keith had the car."

There was a long pause. She finally broke it. "Trust you!"
she said violently.

"All I'm doing is stating the facts. What's more, he didn't
return the car until the Friday. So if he was involved in the
accident, the car was in his possession long enough to have
had the repairs carried out."

"You're calling him a murderer now!"

"The driver involved was not guilty of murder; probably of causing death by dangerous driving and perhaps driving when under the influence."

"Trust you to quibble like a dried-up lawyer," she shouted.

"You're becoming hysterical."

"What d'you expect when you accuse Keith of killing the woman?"

"I haven't. I've merely pointed out what's possible."

"I know what you're really thinking."

"I doubt it. You asked me not to inform the police that Keith had borrowed my car. Did he persuade you to do that?"

"I asked on his behalf because of what would happen otherwise. Now what's going on in your lawyer's mind? You're wondering if I'm lying?"

"Of course I'm not. I can be certain you'd never lie to me any more than I would lie to you."

She looked away. "I'm sorry. I didn't mean what I said."

"Forgotten . . . This is how things are. When Keith confirms he was not involved in the accident and therefore could not have had any cause to have the car repaired I will know the forensic evidence is wrong."

"So what are you going to do?"

"Ask him to confirm."

"That'll just make him think you suspect him."

"He has the common sense to understand and not leap to incorrect conclusions." He was silent for a moment, then said: "There is something more you must understand."

"Well?"

"There is the criminal offence of trying to pervert the

course of justice. It's an offence to lie to the police in order to prevent their arresting someone who has committed a crime. So far, I have not told the whole truth because I know the police are mistaken in believing I was involved and I have every reason to accept that neither was Keith. But if they become convinced that I was involved, they are going to threaten to charge me. Keith has to understand that should this happen, I shall have to tell them the full truth."

"To save your own skin."

"To save your and my future," he said, deeply hurt.

Meyer was walking across the front room when Lipman entered it through one of the far dooways. He called out, then moved into the waiting area, which was empty. "Has Sparrow been questioned yet?" he asked Lipman when the other was within earshot.

"Greg's tracked him down and he swears he never works on doubtful cars. Greg laughed in his face and made him open up the workshop. There's no trace of anything that could lead back to the Astra."

Meyer swore.

"I gather from Bert that Ryan played it very cool when you questioned him and he pointed out all the gaps in the evidence?"

"What else would you expect from a solicitor who's reasonably on the ball?"

"But some of his points were keen?"

"Too bloody keen. As of now, he knows that we know that we haven't a case to take to court."

"Is it worth seeing if the Vauxhall people can help any further?"

"They've confirmed that they cannot specifically

follow through paint or spares supplied to retail points."

"Can we trace a good connection with Randers Cross to explain why he was in that area?"

"He claims they've no friends live near there. How do we prove that a lie? Grab their address book when they're not looking?"

"I suppose there's no chance of identifying the passenger in the car?"

"What's the description? A large man with a craggy face and a full beard. Could it be more useless?"

"The case is looking more and more like a loser."

"That's your opinion," Meyer said angrily.

Lipman stood his ground. "It doesn't seem like one we can win."

"There's still work to do."

"Can we afford to do it? The crime lists for the past week are fuller and will keep us running ragged even though Andy's back from his course and no one's now away sick. Spend more time on trying to nail Ryan and we're going to fall even further behind."

It was the old problem – how did one get the priorities right? . . . "We'll start questioning neighbours to see if they saw the Astra that night."

"The odds against are heavy."

"I don't believe in odds."

"It's over three weeks ago. A prosecution memory that old is usually just a meal for the defence."

"When word gets back to Ryan that we're questioning the neighbours, he's going to start panicking because he can't be certain no one saw him leave or return. Panic could make him lose his cool."

"Not if he's as smart as he sounds."

"If you put as much effort into working out how, instead of explaining why you can't, we might get some-where."

Lipman said, coldly respectful: "I'll detail someone to start questioning the neighbours."

Laura waited for the programme on the building of the pyramids to start before she said: "I must have a word with Margie."

Ryan reached to his side for the cordless phone.

"Don't bother. I'll go out so I don't bother you."

"You won't."

She stood, crossed to his chair, leaned over and very gently and briefly nibbled his left ear. "Whenever I make a phone call, you're always so curious you don't concentrate on what you're watching."

He grinned.

She went upstairs to their bedroom. The phone had a very long cord and she could stand in the doorway to look across the corridor and down above the head of the stairs at the hall. If he left the sitting-room, she would have ample warning. She dialled. When the connection was made, she said: "It's me," absurdly conscious of the breach of grammar because she was making certain her husband didn't overhear her. "The police have been questioning Alan again."

"The penalty of being a gentleman," Tyler said. "So much more fun for the police to hassle."

"Stop trying to sound smart."

"We're very vinegary to-day!"

"It was a detective inspector. They're trying to claim Alan's car has been resprayed and one of the headlights had been replaced."

109

"What did he say to that?"

She noticed the change in his tone, but was too concerned to question the possible significance of this. "He told them they had to be wrong."

He once more spoke lightly. "And their reply was?"

"They could prove what they claimed."

"And the consequence was?"

"Be serious, will you? The police believe it was his car involved in the accident."

"They can't, or they'd have charged him."

"He says they haven't enough evidence to do that yet, but if they ever think they have, he's going to tell them the truth."

"Remind him that they can bluster all they like, provided he stands firm they'll soon enough give up."

"You still don't understand. It'll take hardly anything more to persuade him to tell the truth because with his stupid conscience, he wants to. It's a miracle he hasn't already done so. He's going to ask you directly if there can be any truth in what the police say."

"And I'll answer, none. Being a man of honour, he'll accept my honest assurance."

"The police swear they can prove what they say about the car."

"So you've said."

"Alan's never had that sort of work done to it. So if they're right, it means . . ." She became silent.

"Are you asking me if I had it resprayed because I drove it into the old woman? No, I did not."

"Thank God for that!"

"Are you still a woman of such little faith?"

"I've been terrified that somehow all this would hurt you. I'd go crazy if it did."

110

"We must make certain you never suffer such a fate. A little more wifely encouragement of the more intimate nature might be a good idea. It's remarkable how eager to help that can make a man."

Sixteen

Tyler stepped into the hall. "I came as soon as I could."

"Thanks. Is it too early for a drink?" Ryan asked.

"I can only answer that it's not too late to accept."

They went through to the sitting-room where Laura was seated on the smaller settee. "Hullo, cousin," Tyler said. "You're looking more lovely than ever."

"Very B-movie script," she said.

"Uncalled for. My compliment was sincere and heartfelt."

"You don't know what those words mean."

Tyler laughed, spoke to Ryan. "It's lucky you don't think us enemies, but know the true relationship."

"Indeed. What will you have to drink?"

"Would you have such a thing as a lager?"

"Yes."

"A very broad-minded fellow!"

There were times when Tyler's humour grated more than usual. Ryan asked Laura what she wanted, then went over to the cocktail cabinet, remembered the lager was in the pantry – neither he nor Laura drank it so that Tyler's malicious inference had not been totally unjustified – returned to the sitting-room and poured out the drinks.

Tyler looked across the top of the pewter tankard. "I gather I'm in for a searching interrogation?"

"I do need to discuss something important," Ryan replied, conscious he sounded pompous.

"You want my assurance that you can tell the police to bugger off and bother someone else?"

"Roughly speaking."

Tyler laughed. "You're referring to my choice of verbs? Humble apologies . . . Throughout the time I borrowed your car, I promise you I did not have an accident, I did not hit and kill a woman, I did not have the car resprayed and a damaged headlamp replaced."

"That settles that, then."

"So now you can enjoy life a little more?"

Laura said quickly: "Alan's done so much to help you."

"I know that full well! Sorry, Alan. To tell the truth and shame the devil, I'm just trying to conceal how grateful I really feel. Silly, isn't it, how difficult we English find it to let our emotions see the sky? I'm very aware of the fact that if you hadn't kept your mouth shut, the police would have scooped me up with shouts of joy and called the case closed."

"I rather doubt that," Ryan said quietly.

"But you've had the benefit of respectability; you've no reason to believe the police aren't as devoted to the cause of justice as they proclaim. I, on the other hand, have learned the hard way that their true devotion is to success. I'm sure Laura's told you very little about my past since it embarrasses her so much. But the fact is that when the others asked me to join them in the burglary, I said I'd have nothing to do with violence. They swore there wouldn't be any. But the night watchman surprised us and to shut him up, they used force. They were ready to admit I'd taken no part in that, but the police wouldn't listen as they wanted a clean sweep. So to make certain, they claimed they'd found a homemade cosh on me."

114

"Your lawyers must have raised the question of planted evidence?"

"I couldn't afford anyone, so the state was paying my blokes; people like that won't tackle the prosecution head on for fear that if they do, they'll find they're given less and less work."

A warped judgment, based on the urge to denigrate the system, Ryan thought. "Were you convicted of aggravated assault?"

"That's right. Likely to make things much trickier, isn't it? As I understand things, the police are now saying they can name your car?"

"They claim the forensic evidence proves the Astra has recently been repainted and the headlamp has been replaced. They lack any proof, as far as I can tell, that my car was in a collision, that the collision was with Mrs Yates, that because of damage sustained I had the repairs done in order to hide the damage Despite this, they may well decide to face me and demand answers which will leave me no option other than to tell the truth or lie. If I lie and can be proved to have lied on a point of obvious and vital importance, it will be useless for me to plead emotional and family ties in mitigation; I will be charged with attempting to pervert the course of justice. In these circumstances, then, I am going to have to tell them that you had the car on the night of the accident and until the following Friday."

"Fair enough."

"You do understand?"

"I'd have to be as thick as two planks not to. If it's you or me, it's got to be me."

"I must say, that's not how I should put it. And there is the point that since you were not involved in the accident, my actions can't cause you any distress beyond being questioned."

"But I've told you, if the police . . ." Laura began, her voice shrill.

Tyler interrupted her. "I think it'll be better if I explain. Alan, the hard fact is, it won't just be questioning. They'll exert all the pressure they dare use. It'll be, 'Come on you bastard, you've got a record so it had to be you; prove you weren't driving the car or we've got you; keep on causing us grief and we'll work to have your sentence doubled.'"

"Can't you produce a witness who can say you couldn't have been the driver?"

"No."

"Laura said you were staying at a hotel. Didn't you speak to any member of staff near enough to half past ten that night to do you some good?"

"I told her I was in a hotel when in fact I was in a friend's pad. The reason for that is simple. When I came out of stir, she persuaded me to go straight and backed me to making a success of my life. I've done my best to try to make her understand what her help and faith has meant and means to me. But if I'd told her I'd been staying with Alf, she'd have wanted to know who he was and when I told her, she'd have been scared I was going all the way backwards. I couldn't do that to her when it seemed easy not to."

"Presumably, Alf is an ex-convict."

"And at the same time, a bloke who'll risk his life to save yours. They don't come any truer than him. But the police see things differently. Offer them Alf as an alibi and they'd laugh themselves sick."

Laura faced Ryan. "You've got to do something."

"I've done all I can, which is the point I've been making. And frankly, I don't agree with Keith's pessimistic summation. I'm quite certain that the police in general aren't narrow-mindedly vindictive; there have been cases of planted evidence, but very few. In the main, they do their job as honestly as they can and don't buy apparent success at the expense of injustice."

"How would you know when all you see is the one side and that's through rose tinted glasses?"

Tyler said quietly: "Laura, whether Alan's right or wrong doesn't really matter. The hard fact is, if the police pressure him any harder, of course he has to tell the the truth."

"Why should they do that?"

Ryan answered her. "They may decide that the evidence they have sufficiently implicates my car."

"You've told them it can't."

"It's what they believe that counts. Again, they may uncover something more."

"How can they when it wasn't your car?"

"Evidence can be wrongly interpreted; often because then it will fit a preconceived judgement."

She turned to Tyler. "If Alan tells them you had the car—"

He finished the sentence. "They'll bust a collective gut to land me. And the day I'm charged, Leegate Containers will be working out how to get rid of me because they'll be terrified of waking up one morning and finding the till's empty."

"You'd never do that."

"To them, I'd suddenly be potentially capable of everything from robbing blind beggars to serial murders."

"No," she said wildly.

Ryan, alarmed by her emotional state and trying to calm her fears rather than make her accept the situation, said: "The police's suspicions have been raised through a series of coincidences; even though we have to prepare for worse, it's difficult to think that they actually will take all this any further."

"I'll drink to that," Tyler said as he raised his tankard.

After Tyler left, Ryan returned to the sitting-room. "I'll get back to the office. There's a mountain of work on my desk and Mrs Sommerville was at her most disapproving when I told her I had to come here in the middle of the morning."

"You did mean it, didn't you?" Laura asked urgently. "You won't say anything to the police unless you absolutely have to?"

"I promise you I will not tell them the truth unless that becomes necessary. And if it's any comfort, I think there's a good chance the police will recognise they're making a mistake and withdraw. The reason I needed to speak to Keith and make the situation quite clear is that sometimes one needs to look at things pessimistically."

He kissed her goodbye and made his way to the Astra which he was using to save time. He drove northwards up Yarrow Lane, for once finding it difficult to concentrate on what he was doing. If Tyler were totally committed to an honest life, why had he stayed from the Tuesday to the Friday with a man who was probably an active criminal? Friendship should be strong, but not blind. A criminal would know where a car could be secretly resprayed . . . Tyler had promised; to doubt his word was dishonourable. Yet how could the car have recently been resprayed except when he had had it?

Seventeen

B urrell stepped out of the tiny front garden of No 10 and walked slowly along the pavement to No 12, his mind replaying the previous evening. On his way back from the pub, he'd seen Helen. She'd been waiting at a bus stop with another woman. He'd hurried on, hoping she wouldn't look across the road, but she had. They'd stared at each other for what had seemed stomach-tightening minutes, then she'd looked away and put her arm around the other bitch as she did so. The gesture might have been either one that exposed her need for moral support, or a two-finger salute to him. Either way, it made him want to grab the other bitch by the throat and throttle her because if she were gone, perhaps Helen would return. It had taken him a long time to fall asleep; once asleep, he'd dreamed of Helen. When he'd awoken, the details were lost, but he was certain that he'd been happy with her. He'd cried, hating himself for such weakness.

He opened the wrought-iron gate of No 12 and walked along the short gravel path to the front door, rang the bell. The door was opened by a grey haired woman who wore a pinafore over her frock. He introduced himself. "I'd be grateful if you've the time for a word."

"I don't know . . . Jack!" she called out, flustered and a shade nervous.

She was answered in muffled tones from the room

on her right. A moment later, a man stepped into the small hall.

"He's the police."

"You're Mr—?" Burrell paused.

"Tillett. Jack Tillett. And this is the missus."

"I've a question or two I'd like to ask."

"There ain't nothing wrong, is there?"

"Not that directly concerns you. The thing is, we're conducting an investigation and it's possible you might be able to help us."

"I don't see how. I mean ... I suppose you'd best come in."

Burrell moved inside and shut the door after himself.

"In there," said Tillett, pointing at the door of the room from which he'd come out.

"It's not tidy," she said hurriedly. She spoke directly to Burrell. "With him having retired and home all day, I can't keep things how they ought to be."

"No call for concern, Mrs Tillett. It'll be tidy enough compared to my place, me being on my own." For a reason Burrell had not tried to explain to himself, but could very easily have done so, he had allowed the flat to become a mess. Helen had always kept it in a spick and span condition.

The front room was over-furnished and not nearly as untidy as had been suggested. The television was on. "Turn that off," she said. With obvious reluctance, her husband did so.

They sat. The Tilletts waited uneasily for him to explain the visit.

"I hope what I say to you won't go outside these four walls because it's kind of confidential." The DI had told him to say this to every household to ensure that the details of his visit would be quickly and widely disseminated. "You'll be friendly with the Ryans next door?"

The Tilletts looked at each other. It was she who finally answered. "Depends what you mean. He'll say good morning; she won't say that much."

"It's not quite like that," her husband mildly objected.

"Isn't it?"

"What I mean is, he'll be friendly enough to have a chat."

"But that's the end of it. When did he last ask you into the house for a drink?"

"He's not going to do that."

"Why not? Because he thinks himself too grand?"

Tillett didn't answer.

"And even if he did ask, she'd make you wish you hadn't gone."

Burrell said: "But the long and short of everything is, you can recognise the two of 'em."

"Course we can," she said.

"And would you recognise their cars?"

"Maybe, maybe not. But John knows more about that sort of thing than me."

Tillett said: "It's like this. If I see either of their cars near their place, I know they're theirs. But in the middle of High Street, I wouldn't. You see, they've not got something special, like a Rolls. Once he said to me, he did, for him cars was just a way of moving around."

"So if you saw a car driving away from their house, you'd know if it was theirs?"

"I reckon."

"Did you see the Astra shooting brake on Tuesday evening, the twenty-second of last month, any time after five in the evening?"

"That's a long time ago."

"Just over a month."

121

"It's not all that easy to remember."

"I know. But there's just the chance."

"Why do you want to know if we saw the car?" she asked.

"It might help our inquiries if you did."

"How?"

"I can't really say. I'm just told to go out and ask the questions."

"Seems a funny sort of thing to want to know."

"You'd be surprised what we have to find out . . . So d'you think you saw it then?"

They looked at each other once more, shook their heads.

Burrell stood. "Thanks for your help, then. Sorry to have bothered you."

She looked up. "Know something? The twenty-second was when our Gwen had Ed. Eight and a half pounds. Can't do much better than that, can you?"

"I wouldn't want to if it was me having it."

"If men was to put up with all the pain and trouble of having 'em, they wouldn't be so eager beforehand."

"Steady on, mother," Tillett muttered.

"It's the truth."

"Maybe, but . . . well, not for saying."

"You mean like a pint of beer, but don't want to wash up the glass afterwards."

Burrell left the room, followed by Tillett. As he opened the front door, Tillett said: "She goes on a bit like that."

"A lot of women do."

"As I tell her, we have to put up with just as much, only in a different way. Have to shave each day, don't we? If it's like that for them, why do they go on wanting kids? It's always the women that do."

Except that some women didn't.

"And Mr Ryan ain't really like she makes out. He'll always have a chat. Like when I told him about Gwen just having had Ed; gave her his best wishes, he did."

"How's that?"

Tillett was clearly startled by the sharpness of the question.

Burrell reached past the other to close the front door to cut off the cold, damp air. "You spoke to Mr Ryan on the twenty-second?"

"Did I? I suppose I must have done. I mean that was when we heard from Gwen."

"Tell me about it."

"I was walking down to Sainsbury to see if it was still open and to buy a bottle of their champagne to wet the baby's head for when Gwen's Charlie called in."

"It was in the evening, then?"

"That's right. We didn't hear from Charlie at the hospital until after dark. The waiting had Phyllis real worried. I kept telling her, it'll be all right. And it was. Eight and a half pounds."

The door of the front room opened and Mrs Tillett came out; Burrell stepped back to afford her more room.

"I was saying how Mr Ryan was glad to hear Gwen had had Esmeralda." Tillett's tone became a shade challenging. "He was very interested to hear."

"Maybe," she said.

"What time of the evening would this have been?" Burrell asked.

"Can't rightly say," Tillett answered.

"When does the supermarket close?"

She said: "On Tuesdays, at eight."

"So how close to eight d'you reckon we're talking about?"

"The place was closing when I got there and they didn't want to let me in. But I told 'em about Gwen and they did."

"How long would it have taken you to walk there?"

"Near enough, ten minutes."

"Where did you have this chat with Mr Ryan?"

"In front of his garage."

"Did you now? So you probably saw his cars?"

"That's right."

"They were both there?"

"As far as I could tell. Only—"

"Yes?"

"It's just I remember thinking they both looked like saloons instead of one of 'em being a shooting brake and the other – if you see what I mean – looked all new and posh and I wondered if he'd bought himself something smart at last."

Burrell thanked them, left. As he returned to the CID Escort, he thought that the DI was going to find it difficult whether or not to welcome this evidence.

Meyer stared axross his desk at Burrell. "Could he have the dates all cocked up?"

"Not with going out to buy the champagne. The wife confirms things."

"And he's doubtful about seeing the Astra in the garage?"

"Doubtful, but nothing stronger."

Meyer leaned back in his chair. "This goes a long way to confirming what's been on the cards for some time. He lent the Astra to a friend who had the accident, so he's doing his damnedest to cover for the friend. Small wonder he can say he was home all evening and sound truthful and the wife can back him up without a blink . . .

Did you try to find out anything more about the second saloon car?"

"I reckoned you'd want to do that so I left it alone."

"Good thinking ... Maybe, just maybe, we've had the break that's going to crash this case wide open."

The phone in the hall rang and Ryan looked round for the cordless one.

"It's probably in the dining-room," Laura said.

He stood, left the room, and lifted the receiver of the phone in the hall.

"Mr Ryan?"

"Speaking."

"It's Jack here; Jack Tillett."

"Good evening."

"I thought ... That is, we reckoned you'd be interested to hear we had a detective along, asking questions about you."

"How very surprising!"

"As I said to Phyllis, you ought to know what's going on."

"That's very thoughtful of you. What seemed to be concerning him?"

"He started off by asking if we knew you. Of course we did, I told him. Then he wanted to know if we'd seen your car on the twenty-second of last month. It's a long time ago, I said. But then I remembered that that's the evening I met you just after we heard Gwen's kid had arrived. You'll recollect me telling you?"

"Of course."

"I was on my way to buy some champagne for when Charlie called in after seeing Gwen and the new arrival."

"So what happened when you told the detective about this?"

"He wanted to know about your cars. Seemed a real odd thing to ask."

"Could you make out exactly what interested him about them?"

"Not really, except he had been asking earlier if we knew your Astra by sight. Depends where I see it, I said."

"Presumably you told him both my wife's Rover and my Astra were in the garages?"

"Well, no, not as a matter of fact."

"Why's that?"

"One of 'em didn't look like your shooting brake; more like a smart saloon . . . No offence intended," he added hastily.

"How very interesting."

"In what way?"

"That you should think the shooting brake wasn't there and some other car was. Of course, since we were talking, you could only have given it a cursory glance."

"That's right," Tillett said very quickly, eager to deny any suggestion that he had not been giving Ryan his full attention.

"And the street lighting isn't all that good. It's strange how shapes become so distorted in poor light."

"It was your old car after all?"

"Haven't you seen it around since then?" Ryan laughed. "As I think I once said to you, I'm no car buff and I can't see any reason for changing one until it ceases to work reliably."

"D'you think . . . well, ought I to get in touch with the police and tell 'em I must have made a mistake?"

"It's not worth your bother. But if they ever do get back on to you, you might as well just mention that fact."

126

"I'll certainly do that."

"Good. Is your granddaughter well?"

"Couldn't be better. Gwen's thinking about the christening."

"I'm sure she is. You must allow us to give her a small christening present."

"That's very kind of you, Mr Ryan. Gwen will be real chuffed."

"A pleasure. And I'm grateful to you for having bothered to tell me what's been happening. I may well decide to speak to the police and tell them that if they wish to know something which concerns me, they should get directly in touch with me and not bother other people." He said goodbye, replaced the receiver.

He stared across the hall at the oil painting of his great-great-grandfather in a typical Victorian paterfamilias pose. It was only a short time since he had warned Laura always to expect the unexpected. He'd not expected to be proved so right, so quickly.

He returned to the sitting-room.

"Who was it?" she asked, without looking away from the television.

"Jack Tillett."

"Who's he?"

"Our next-door neighbour on the left."

"That little man with a barmaid of a wife? What on earth did he want?"

He sat. "Their daughter's just produced. I said we'd like to give the child a christening present so will you look out for something."

"What an extraordinary thing to do! If you're not damned careful, you'll have them coming in for a chat."

"You're going to have to be friendly."

"Like hell!"

"There's going to be a very great deal riding on their goodwill."

"I can't imagine why."

"Regard someone as a friend and you're very reluctant to drop him into the mud."

"What are you talking about?"

"The police have been asking him if he saw my car on the twenty-second of last month."

She used the remote control to switch off the television. "They've no right to ask those sort of people questions about us."

After several years of marriage, she could still astonish him by the degree of her snobbery. "They're investigating a fatal accident. That gives them the right to question anyone who they can reasonably believe may be able to help them.

"The little man next door certainly can't do that."

"When I was walking home that Tuesday, I met him outside our garages."

"So?"

"When he looked into the yard, he saw two saloon cars, yours and the BMW. That made him wonder if I'd bought a new car. It will hardly need much imagination on the part of the police to work out that I lent my car to someone who left his in the garage, and it was this someone who had the accident."

"Oh, my God!"

"They may well decide they now have enough evidence to charge me – their objective, obviously, to force me to identify the driver."

"But you mustn't," she said wildly.

"As I've said several times, both to you and Keith, if the circumstances demand that, I shall have to. But there is just a chance that we won't reach that position. I've done what

128

I can – which includes the promised christening present – to persuade Tillett he must have made a mistake when he thought he saw a saloon and not a shooting brake. Hopefully, when the police question him in greater detail, his evidence will have become too indecisive to be of any value to them."

"I hope to God you succeeded."

He was sadly certain that she gave no thought to the fact that for her he had yet again betrayed his principles by trying to make someone change his evidence.

Eighteen

As Burrell rang the door bell of No 12, Meyer watched a robin alight on the high brick wall that marked the grounds of Ragstone Hall. It regarded him with head tilted slightly to one side. Curiosity or fear?

The door was opened by Tillett. "Hullo, you again!"

"That's right," Burrell said. "And this is Detective Inspector Meyer."

"Pleased to meet you," said Tillett uncertainly.

Meyer moved forward to shake hands. A friendly beginning could make for a productive ending. "Just a few points to go over which maybe you can help us on. Shouldn't bother you for long."

"It's no bother. The wife's out shopping and the ground's too wet to do any gardening so there's only the telly. Come on in, gentlemen."

They went into the front room and were offered tea or coffee. Meyer chose coffee, Burrell didn't want either. As Tillett left the room, Meyer picked up a copy of the *Daily Mirror* and skimmed through the headlines. "Arsenal's getting a new manager."

Burrell remained silent.

"What team do you support?"

"Can't say I'm interested in football."

Was he interested in anything? Meyer wondered. Perhaps

his wife had been justified in leaving him. It was a pity she had not done so for a man.

Tillett returned. He put the tray down, handed a mug to Meyer. "Help yourself so as you have exactly what you want."

Meyer discussed the latest political scandal as he added sugar and milk to the coffee, then directed the conversation to the night of the twenty-second. "I gather your daughter has just had a child?"

"She weighed eight and a half pounds. And her eyes are blue like our Gwen's—"

Meyer restrained his impatience for as long as possible, which wasn't for very long, then interrupted a description of how she had gurgled at her grandmother. "We're in a bit of a rush so if you don't mind, we'll move on. You and Mr Ryan had a chat on the pavement and the garage gates were open?"

"That's right."

"And during the chat, you looked across the yard and saw two cars, both of 'em saloons?"

Tillett hesitated.

"Isn't that what you said to Constable Burrell?"

On cue, Burrell nodded.

"Yes, but—"

"Well?"

"I'm not really all that certain."

"About what exactly?"

"Well, it's like this. I just glanced at 'em quickly since I was talking to Mr Ryan and the light's not so good because the nearest street lamp's some way away and there's lots of shadows. Makes things look different."

"But hardly sufficiently different to cause confusion between the lumpy, square cut rear of a shooting brake

132

and the shaped lines of a sloping rear window and a boot."

Tillett moved uneasily in his chair.

"Are you now saying that you can't be certain that there were two saloons in the garages and not one saloon and one shooting brake?"

"I . . . well, I suppose I am."

"Are you even certain there were two cars?"

He missed the sarcasm. "There were definitely two."

"You're confusing me. A moment ago you were not really looking and the light was so poor, now you're saying you can be certain there were two cars which means you did take careful note of them."

"No, it doesn't."

"I'm afraid it does."

"But . . . They was reflecting what light there was and so I could see the two reflections in the two garages."

"Didn't the pattern of reflected light tell you what kind of shape each car had."

"No."

At a sign from Meyer, Burrell took up the questioning. "Mr Tillett, you must have judged at the time that they were both saloons or you wouldn't have said they were to me."

"But when I thought about it, I couldn't be certain. I mean, I wasn't concentrating on what I was looking at."

"The shapes are very different from the back, like the inspector said."

"Not in shadow."

"Don't you reckon first impressions are best? Maybe asking yourself questions has raised doubts that don't really exist?"

"I just don't know."

"Suppose I asked you what you think is most likely, what

would your answer be – two saloons or one saloon and one shooting brake?"

"I can't say."

Meyer, his tone noticeably sharper, said: "Have you spoken to Mr Ryan since yesterday and told him you'd been asked questions by us?"

"Well, I . . . I did ring him to mention it. I mean, we're neighbours, so I thought he should know."

"And I imagine he told you that it was his shooting brake in the garage, not a second saloon?"

"In a way."

"In what way?"

"He said he hadn't bought a new car."

"Did he try to explain why you made the mistake?"

"He pointed out that the light was so poor, it was easy to go wrong."

"And he probably added that since you were talking to him, you wouldn't have been concentrating on the cars in the garages?"

"Something like that, I suppose."

Meyer stood. "He should be very grateful to you."

"How d'you mean?"

"Think about it." He led the way out.

Burrell was driving the CID Escort and as he accelerated away from the pavement, Meyer said angrily: "Why the hell didn't you get a written statement yesterday before Ryan got at him?"

"I thought you'd want to question him and—"

"You didn't bloody well think."

Yesterday it had been 'Good thinking'; today, it was, 'Didn't bloody well think'. Burrell gained a perverse satisfaction from the injustice.

*   *   *

Mrs Sommerville looked into the office. "Sorry to interrupt you, Mr Ryan, but Detective Inspector Meyer says he needs to speak to you."

"Tell him I feel no such compulsion."

The client, who dressed as if in clothes borrowed from a scarecrow, yet who owned and efficiently farmed nearly a thousand acres, laughed. "There aren't many of us lead lives so honest we can tell the police to shove off."

And, Ryan thought grimly, he wasn't one of them. Yet he had to find the dividing line between an eager willingness to co-operate, which could suggest guilt, and a refusal to co-operate, which could suggest guilt. "I suppose you'd better tell him I'll see him when possible. But add that I'm very pressed for time."

She left.

It was nearly twenty minutes before Meyer and Burrell entered the room. "It's kind of you to find the time to see us," Meyer said.

"Glad to give any help I can," Ryan replied with equal insincerity. He pointed to the two chairs in front of the desk. "What's the problem this time?" he asked as he sat.

"I doubt we really have to explain," Meyer said pleasantly.

"There is a rule of evidence which says that nothing can be assumed and everything must be detailed, hence the judge who asks 'What is a pop star' to the sarcastic amusement of journalists."

"Then I will detail the facts. We can now be certain your Astra shooting brake was not in the garage in Ragstone Hall on the night of Tuesday, the twenty-second of last month—"

"I know nothing of your certainties."

"Mr Tillett, your next-door neighbour, met you outside your garage entrance that evening. He looked across the yard and saw two saloon cars, not one saloon and one shooting brake."

"He did mention to me that that's what he'd suggested to a detective. But he added that the circumstances being what they were, second thoughts convinced him that he could have been so easily mistaken that he probably was."

"First impressions are usually right."

"A dubious proposition."

"Do you know why they were right in this instance?"

"I know they were wrong."

"His first impressions were formed before he was cleverly brainwashed into accepting that he could have been wrong."

"Really?"

"He phoned you after Constable Burrell had spoken to him yesterday, didn't he?

"Yes."

"And after you'd heard what he had to say, you carefully pointed out that the light in the yard is poor, there are many shadows, and it is very easy to confuse shapes."

"Whether or not I did say all that seems immaterial since it has to be common sense."

"You also persuaded him he could not have looked carefully at the two cars because he was talking to you and would not have wanted to seem uninterested in what you were saying."

"He thinks that? Then I fear he may believe me to be somewhat presumptuous."

"You deny mentioning that possibility to him?"

"I certainly don't remember doing so."

"You seem to have either a poor or a very selective memory."

"I must leave you to decide which."

"Suppose he did see, as he first stated, two saloon cars, what would that suggest?"

"He was mistaken."

"It would suggest you lent your car to someone who'd left his car in your garage."

"Suggestions need a measure of reasonable possibility to have any relevance."

"And this someone drank too much and was driving your shooting brake when it hit Mrs Yates, threw her against the door of the car with such force that she suffered injuries from which she later died."

There was a silence. Finally, Meyer said: "You've no comment?"

"I'm sorry. I was waiting for further fanciful suggestions."

"You're a lawyer, meant to be supporting justice. You're doing everything you can to deny justice by protecting a friend. I suppose living in a large house, enjoying the luxuries of life, it's never once occurred to you that Yates's life has been shattered by his wife's death. Perhaps you even believe that people like them don't have feelings and that gives you the right to protect this friend?"

"Do you usually introduce a strong political slant into your interrogations?"

"I'm just wondering if you are capable of seeing your actions in the same light as I do."

"That's unlikely. I'm concerned with facts."

"Your only concern seems to be to save a drunken driver from the consequences of his own crime."

"Inspector, we could continue this conversation *ad nauseam* since it would be hard to find anything on which we agree, but I am a very busy man."

"Was your Astra shooting brake in your garage at ten

twenty-five on the night of Tuesday, the twenty-second of last month?"

"Since we were at home, presumably it must have been."

"Why only presumably?"

"I will not have gone out to the garage to make certain it was still there."

"Was a friend staying with you at that time?"

"No."

"Did a friend leave his car with you?"

"I have already answered that."

"You have carefully not been answering any of my questions because if you can avoid committing yourself to a lie, it'll be relatively difficult to prove you've set out to pervert the course of justice."

"It's always difficult to prove something that's incorrect."

They left, without even a curt goodbye. Their angry frustration, Ryan decided, was probably an optimistic sign. Optimistic? If he'd been asked a couple of months before whether he could find satisfaction in knowing justice was being defeated, he would have found the question insulting.

"He's a smooth customer," Burrell said, as he drove down to the left-hand corner beyond the DIY store which had replaced the corn exchange many years before.

"He's a lawyer." Meyer spoke with contempt.

"What happens now?"

"You concentrate on the driving to give us a chance of returning safely."

"Sir," said Burrell flatly.

Meyer had always criticised seniors who worked out their irritation on their juniors, yet here he was, doing just that. Frustration. The certainty that he knew, but lacked the ability to prove; the knowledge that a guilty man might stay free

138

because misplaced loyalty was so strong. "We'll draw up a report for the CPS and let them decide whether there are sufficient grounds for arresting Ryan."

Burrell accepted the verbal olive branch. "Do you still think that if he's actually charged, he'll start talking?"

"How many friendships are strong enough for self-sacrifice?"

When Ryan returned home, Laura was in the sitting-room, working on her latest needlework – a flower pattern with subtle shading that called for fine stitches. He crossed and kissed her on the cheek. "I had a couple of detectives at the office," he said, as he straightened up.

She held her right hand still, the needle just above the linen. "What did they want?"

"To panic me by claiming Tillett had definitely identified two saloons in our garages. I stonewalled to the point where the inspector accused me of trying to save a drunken driver from the consequences of his crime." He hoped she would finally show that she appreciated how much it hurt him to have to face such an accusation.

"But you weren't panicked?"

"No."

"What is it? You're surely not thinking it could have been Keith?"

"It could have been. Whether I think it was is another matter—"

"Just because he's not completely strait-laced like you, hasn't led a blameless life, doesn't worship authority—"

In turn, he interrupted her. "We've been through all this before."

"He did not have anything to do with the accident."

He hoped that he would not be forced to tell the police

139

the truth because then he would find out if she were right or wrong.

Meyer, standing by his desk, read the brief report for a second time. He swore aloud. Parker entered the room as the last four letter word rode the air waves. "Something wrong?" he asked with sly innocence.

Meyer put the sheet of paper down on the desk, jammed his hands in his pockets, stamped over to the window and looked out at the wall of rain which had been falling since dawn. "You're an insolent bastard!"

"Me, sir? Never."

Meyer turned, crossed to the desk, sat. "The CPS says there's insufficient evidence to charge Ryan. They express their surprise that the investigating office failed to realise that there is no evidence hard enough to tie in the Astra with the accident. I explained Ryan should be charged, to open up the case, but in their infinite wisdom, they ignored that."

"The idea's too subtle for them. So what happens now?"

"We sit and twiddle our thumbs, hoping something more turns up, knowing it won't."

Nineteen

It seemed winter might have become endless. Since November, there had been record rainfall, dense fogs and heavy snowfalls. However, on the fourteenth of February – and what more suitable date could there have been? – the weak sun shone out of a clear sky to offer the optimistic hope that there would be a summer again.

Laura left her car in the municipal car park, despite the fact that the block of flats had its own generous parking space. If the Rover were recognised by someone who knew her, an explanation that she had been shopping would sound perfectly reasonable. As she walked along the pavements and then up the rise, she experience a familiar sense of tension. She wished she could understand why Tyler possessed such power to excite her; previously, it had always been she who had excited when, and only when, she so wished. Once, she had tried to resist him and reassert herself, but the attempt had failed and merely provoked his amusement.

She reached the block of flats and took the lift up to the top floor. She crossed to the door on the left of the landing, rang the bell. She'd asked him for a key; he'd refused on the grounds that there must always be the chance her husband would find it and then even his naïve loyalty wouldn't be sufficient to prevent his wondering what lock it fitted. For days after this refusal, she'd tormented herself with the thought that what he'd feared had been her entering unannounced to find him screwing another woman.

He opened the door and she went in; he kissed her with a luxuriant skill that seemed to stroke almost every nerve in her body. He said that first they'd have a drink to celebrate a reunion delayed by the bad weather, knowing how she'd hate the wait. He played her emotions with the skill of a virtuoso and the pleasure of a sadist . . .

Later, as they lay naked on top of the bedclothes, pleasantly warm because the heating was set high, he amused himself by alerting her passion once more, then stopping as if from boredom before it became fully aroused. "Has there been any sign of the police?"

"Not since they saw Alan in his office and told him what that ghastly little erk who lives next door had told them . . . Can't we forget all that?"

He didn't answer.

"Stop doing that."

"And deny you the pleasure? . . . Since it's roughly six weeks ago, we can declare the emergency over. These days, the police are kept so busy that they can't track a case for very long unless it's really high profile. The media made a fuss because the old woman had won a medal, but it was only a two-day wonder."

"Kiss me."

"Patience."

She gripped him and kissed him.

He used his fingers to make her cry out. "I said, 'patience'."

"That hurt, you bastard!"

"Pleasure has to be touched with pain if it's to become absolute." He reached out with his fingers again, but this time she was ready for the movement and she slapped his hand away with such force that momentum carried her hand forward to strike him on the cheek. Surprise caused him to cry out.

She giggled. "So what's that done for your absolute?"

When she arrived home, Ryan's car was parked in the right-hand garage. Shit! she said silently. She lowered the passenger's sun visor and leaned over to examine her reflection in the small mirror on the reverse side, searching for any sign that could betray the past few hours.

In the hall, she called Ryan's name and the muffled answer came from the library-cum-study. She went through and as she entered, he looked up from the computer. "Hullo, darling," she said. She kissed him warmly.

"I wondered where you'd got to."

"Didn't you see my note on the hall table?"

"There wasn't one."

"Are you sure?"

"Quite positive."

"I was going to write one so you'd know where I was and not worry."

"You've obviously been to hell."

She knew sudden panic. "Why d'you say that?"

"The road to hell is paved with good intentions."

The relief was as great as had been the panic. "You really can be absurd."

"Surely a welcome change from my normal serious sapient self?"

"I love you all kinds." She kissed him again, then moved back to stand close to the desk. "You're home very early?"

"When I got back from seeing a client in Peascroft, I needed to collect some work I'd started here over the weekend and decided it would make more sense to stay on rather than return to the office ... And you, no doubt, have been shopping?"

"Margie rang and suggested I went over and had a light lunch with her. I did look at the shops on the way back, but didn't buy anything so you can breathe easily."

He used a pencil to underline several words on the page that lay by the side of the keyboard. "You've been seeing a lot of her recently."

"No, I haven't; this is the first time since the last blizzard. Anyway, why not? We're old friends."

"I know, but ... if I were you, I'd be cautious."

"How d'you mean?"

"In not becoming too emotionally involved. She's always struck me as someone who's basically undependable."

"You only think that because she teases you for being so old fashioned."

He smiled. "From her, that's a compliment. What I'm really trying to say is that when the chips are down, she'll always look after her own interests at the expense of anyone else's."

"Isn't that the norm?"

"I hope not."

"How she'd laugh to hear you say that in all solemnity."

"I expect she would."

"Don't worry, my sweet. I know her well enough never to rely on her."

"I'm glad."

Margie often said how much she envied her for having married the perfect husband – blind to possibilities.

Twenty

The details of the planned raid in south-western Atswitch were given in the conference room in divisional HQ. The detective sergeant, from time to time referring to the street map or the sketch tacked on the display board, detailed each man's movements. The seven PCs and DCs hid their yawns. At the conclusion, the DI addressed them. "OK, you know how it should go. But it won't, because there's always a cock-up. So drill it into your skulls that the order of priority is Lister, papers, other workers, vehicles and parts of vehicles. Lister's been known to carry a shooter, so two members of the armed unit will be joining us. If guns do start, back off. I don't want anyone trying to imitate a hero."

Someone laughed sarcastically.

"Any questions? Any problems?"

No one spoke.

"Assemble at seventeen hundred hours for take-off at eighteen-thirty."

Until the sixties, Atswitch had had a market, noted for the quality of the calves sold there – every Tuesday, veal producers from several nearby counties had travelled to it. To meet the need for transport, a branch line from the station had been built and this had had to cross Flinders Dip, a fold in the land that was a geological curiosity. In the sixties the market had closed for several reasons, the main one being the value of the land to developers. The branch line had been scrapped and the viaduct had become a very short one-way road, the space within the six arches being converted into working areas.

The police divided into two groups and approached number 5 archway from opposite sides. Radio silence was maintained until the DI gave the order to go in. Doors proved to be unlocked and only two men were working inside. There wasn't a gun in sight.

There were three Mercedes, one BMW, and two Jaguars; one of the Mercedes was having its chassis and engine number plates altered. At the southern end of the area was a small, crudely walled-in cubicle in which were car papers being prepared with new identity numbers. It proved to be a fruitful operation.

Lister and his solicitor, newly summoned from home, sat in the interview room on the opposite side of the table to the DI and a DC.

The DI switched on the tape recorder, identified himself, gave the date, the time, and the names of the others present. He listed what had been found in the workshop and asked Lister if he would like to explain the circumstances? The solicitor said his client had nothing to say other than that he could not understand why he had been brought to the police station to suffer an interrogation. He was an honest man who worked very hard to earn an honest living . . . One of the Mercedes had already been identified as a stolen vehicle, how did Lister explain its presence in his workshop? His client had no idea it had been stolen; had he so much as suspected the possibility, he would not have touched it . . . Why had its original identifying plates been removed and new ones – bearing false numbers – prepared for affixing?

His client had not removed anything . . . Then where had the old plates, lying on the ground near the Mercedes, come from? No comment . . . Did Lister think it possible that any of the other cars had been stolen? His client had no reason to think so . . . Could Lister explain why amongst the papers in the office had been one which identified the BMW, but carried numbers completely different from those which, when new, the BMW had been issued? His client would like the chance to have a brief consultation . . .

"The recorder is now being switched off," said the detective inspector, "in order that Mr Lister may confer with his solicitor. DC Arkwright and myself will be leaving the interview room." He flicked up two of the switches. "Bang on the door when you're ready." He led the way out.

The door was banged twenty-three minutes later. The detectives returned, the DI switched on the tape recorder.

"Just a moment," said the solicitor who, if reincarnated, would undoubtedly return as a weasel. "Maybe we could have a chat off the record?"

The DI switched off the tape recorder.

"My client admits nothing. However, he does accept that there would seem to be some circumstantial evidence against him and in the event of being tried on a charge of receiving and selling stolen vehicles, it might be held that he was guilty."

"With the evidence we'll be taking to court, you can change 'might' to 'will'."

"That has to be a matter of conjecture."

"Only to a raving optimist. Just what is the point of all this?"

"My client feels that, finding himself in a certain situation, it may well be advisable to . . . how should I put it?"

"Plead guilty."

The solicitor fidgeted with the corner of his briefcase that

147

was on the table. "You cannot, of course, promise any definite advantage to my client in return for him assisting you with the investigation."

"True enough."

"But if the court is informed he has assisted, it may well show leniency when sentencing?"

"It happens."

"So if my client were to provide a few names—?"

"If he helps us trace the lines into and out of his place, I'll do what's allowed to see the court's notified about how helpful he's been."

Two hours later, Lister said: "That's it."

The DI shook his head. "Not yet. What's the name of the big man behind the buying?"

"I don't know, straight. Chauffeurs come for the cars and hand over the gravy. They don't say who they're working for and I don't ask."

"Are they supposed to guess what to collect and how much to pay you?"

"Someone phones and sorts things out first."

"Now we're making a little progress. Who's he?"

"Like I said, I don't know nothing more. This bloke talks, I listen."

"So how were you introduced?"

"I was doing a bit of quick work and he heard about it and was on the blower asking if I'd like a regular line."

"When does he call you?"

"There ain't no saying. The phone rings and it's him."

The DI made a mental note to arrange for the phone in the workshop to be manned and for a call trace to be set up even though this would probably be a waste of time; if the caller were even half smart, he'd use a different stolen mobile each time.

"That's straight," said Lister urgently.

The DI recognised his expression must falsely have suggested sharp disbelief. Doubt might yet pluck out a little more information. "You're giving me only half the story."

"It's all there. I swear it is, on me mother's grave."

"Like as not you've no idea where that is."

"You can't drop me in the shit just because I don't know no more."

"It can be a rough world. The court may decide you haven't really been all that helpful after all."

Lister hesitated, then said: "Suppose I was to open up on something else?" He lowered his voice. "Would that do some good?"

"Depends what we're talking about."

"It was in all the papers."

"What was?"

"The old woman with some sort of medal what was knocked down by a hit-and-run last year."

The DI could not identify the case beyond the fact that it had not happened in his division. "Carry on."

"He brought the car, wanting the damage rubbed out then and there. I told him, I wasn't doing casual no more. But we was from some time back and he was offering a big fistful. So I did the job and it left looking better than the day it was bought." There was brief pride in his voice. "Put in a new lamp unit, 'cause the glass in the old one got smashed."

"What's his name?"

"No, Guv. We go back a long way and I ain't shopping him. But I can give you the number of the car."

Even after many years in the job, the DI could still be astonished by the convoluted way in which a criminal's mind worked.

Twenty-One

P arker stepped inside the office. " 'Morning, sir. Lovely day."

Meyer said sourly: "It's raining for the fourth day running, last month's crime rate rose, I have to spend the afternoon at county HQ, and my daughter has tonsillitis. It's a bloody awful day."

"I'm about to bring sunshine into your life."

"And I'm about to bust you back into the uniform branch."

"We've just had a call from Atswitch CID. A day or two ago they hauled in a bloke who's been singing like a diva sitting on a needle. Last October, an old pal of his turned up with a car that had been in an accident and needed a new headlamp, a little bit of panel bashing, and a new paint job."

"The Astra shooting brake?"

"None other."

Meyer leaned back in his chair. "So 'the mills of God do grind slowly, yet grind exceeding small.' "

Mrs Sommerville said: "Detective Inspector Meyer and Detective Sergeant Lipman are here and demanding to speak to you right away."

Ryan knew sudden, sharp concern.

"I said it wasn't convenient, but they're insistent. Sir Joseph is due in just over a quarter of an hour."

"I suppose I'll have to see them. If they should still be here when Sir Joseph arrives, ask him to be kind enough to wait; murmur something about a sudden emergency. He's an easygoing type so he should remain calm."

She left. He tried – and naturally failed – to work out why the detectives had returned after so many weeks had passed.

She showed them into the room and set a second chair in front of the desk. "Don't forget you have a very important meeting on the hour, Mr Ryan," she said, staring hard at Meyer as she spoke.

"Thanks for reminding me."

She left.

"I'm not certain whether you know Sergeant Lipman," Meyer said.

"Frankly, nor am I," Ryan managed a brief smile. "I seem to have met a number of your companions in past months . . . Do sit down. And I'm sorry if I have to rush you along rather, but as you heard, time is short."

"It's rather up to you how long we're here."

"That's a cryptic remark."

"Not intentionally."

Lipman ostentatiously brought a notebook out of his coat pocket, uncapped a ballpoint pen, and prepared to write.

"The fact is, we've very recently received some information which concerns you.

"Indeed." Ryan tried to sound only politely interested.

"A man has been arrested for dealing in stolen luxury cars. He was changing identifying numbers, repairing or touching up if necessary, and providing false documents. Interestingly, it seems that the majority of these cars end up in Poland and

Russia. Countries which don't readily come to mind when it's a case of buying luxury cars. Wouldn't you agree?"

"I've never considered the matter."

"But apparently, there's plenty of money in the hands of criminals in the two countries. So now if you see a Mercedes or Jaguar on the roads in Moscow or Warsaw, the owner is far more likely to be a local mafia boss than a restored archduke."

"I don't see how all this can possibly concern me."

"I apologise. It was just an irrelevant comment on the odd way in which values can turn turtle – people doing things you'd never expect them to. To get back on track, before he entered that trade, he made his money ringing cars and by reputation was brilliant at the job. By now, you'll have realised where this is leading?"

"No."

"I'll have to be more specific. In October of last year, he was asked to erase all signs of contact suffered by a dark blue Vauxhall Astra shooting brake. The damage consisted of a broken headlamp, very light ruffling of the surrounding bodywork, and light marks of contact. He replaced the headlight, tapped out the ruffling so expertly it's virtually impossible to detect that the work has been done, and repainted the whole car. Does all this sound very familiar?"

"Is it supposed to?"

"It was your car."

"Impossible."

"We have the sworn statement of the man who carried out the work."

"He's a criminal and therefore totally unreliable."

"Criminals can sing in tune."

"Even assuming he has at some time done such work, it cannot have been on my car."

153

"Being a curious man, he made a note of the registration number. It's that of your Astra."

"Obviously – for a reason I can't begin to suggest – he's trying falsely to implicate me."

"You're a hard fighter," Meyer said with faint and unwilling admiration. "But you're more than intelligent enough to know there comes a point when to fight on is ridiculous. We can now prove it was your car which struck Mrs Yates and caused injuries from which she subsequently died."

There was a long silence.

"I don't believe you were driving that car at the time of the accident. I think you lent it to someone who left his, or perhaps her, saloon car with you. It was that person who drove into Mrs Yates. Will you name the person?"

"What if I do not?"

"Obviously, I arrest you."

"You are attempting to blackmail me."

" 'Blackmail' is a very emotive word, especially when a policeman's involved. Should you be using it to serve your further interests in court, I think you should know that while Sergeant Lipman has been making notes, he has also been recording all that has been said on a tape recorder . . ."

"Hidden."

"Which will not necessarily negate the evidence it holds. Mr Ryan, take the time to understand that I am giving you the chance to avoid being charged with a very serious criminal offence."

Ryan finally accepted the point had been reached at which it was ridiculous to continue to try to fight. Now all he could do was prevent Laura's learning the truth through news of Tyler's arrest; he had to be the one to explain as sympathetically as possible what had happened. "Are you prepared to wait until tomorrow for my answer?"

"Why?"

"That will become clear tomorrow. The only reason for asking is to make things a little easier for a third party."

"If you're thinking of doing something silly . . ."

"You have my word, Inspector."

Meyer noted Lipman's smile of derision and although it was not that which decided him, it did occur to him that it might be a salutary lesson for the detective sergeant to learn that there were still those whose standards were very different from his own. "Very well." He stood. "I shall expect you at the station at eleven o'clock. You may like to have a legal adviser with you."

"On the basis that a doctor should not diagnose his own appendicitis?"

He led the way out of the room.

Ryan slumped back in the chair. Time and again, Tyler had lied. Because of those lies, Laura's pain must be all the greater; because of those lies, he had betrayed his own principles . . .

There was a knock on the door and Mrs Sommerville entered. "You haven't forgotten Sir Joseph, have you? He's already been waiting quite a long time."

"I . . . Tell him I'm very sorry, but I can't see him. Ask him if he'd like to speak to one of the other partners; if not, arrange another appointment."

Her concern was immediate. "Do you need a doctor?"

"There's no doctor clever enough to cure the past."

He walked up Yarrow Lane to Ragstone Hall. The first set of wooden gates were closed and he carried on to the metal gate which he noticed was showing signs of rust on the top left-hand corner. Carrington, looking like a gnome, was working amongst the far belt of trees.

Laura was in the dining-room, talking to Mrs Catlin. Mrs Catlin's expression said she was listening, but not hearing.

"Can we have a word?" he said.

"What about?" She sounded exasperated.

"Let's go through to the library."

Laura turned to Mrs Catlin. "Please do it as I've said."

"If you insist."

They went through to the library. "That woman will drive me crazy," she said. "She will not do things the way I want her to."

"I've—"

She interrupted him. "I want the table polished with the grain. Getting her to understand why seems impossible. D'you think she's deliberately stupid?"

"It's possible. That's the standard defence of the employed."

"If I could find someone else, I would."

"Laura, I've come back because I'm afraid I've some bad news."

"Oh!" She looked quickly at him, then away. She reached out fractionally to straighten the leather bound blotter on the desk.

"I've just had the police along."

"What do they want now, for God's sake?"

"They say they've new evidence in the Yates case."

"Why bother you about it?"

"They can now prove that it was my car which was involved."

Her voice became shrill. "Of course they can't. They're lying."

"They've identified who repaired and repainted it and he's admitted doing all the work."

"You know they're lying. Or can't you believe a policeman would lie, with your ridiculous respect for authority? I'll bet you didn't say a thing to them except yes, sir, no, sir, whatever you say, sir."

"Do you realise what this means?"

"Yes. You've as much backbone as a jellyfish."

"Keith was driving my car when it hit that woman."

"He's told you again and again that he wasn't."

"He must have been."

"This is wonderful! You refuse to realise the police must be lying because you rush to believe Keith is. Just proves how much you hate him."

"Try to look at things less emotionally—"

"You expect me to be unemotional when you're accusing Keith simply because you hate him?"

"I do not hate him. I've told you that God knows how many times. But we just have to accept that he's been repeatedly lying to us in order to persuade us to cover up for him."

"It's only you who needs persuading. I've known from the beginning that the accident was nothing to do with him."

"In view of the latest evidence that it was definitely my car which hit Mrs Yates—"

"To hell with what they're trying to say."

". . . Keith was driving it."

"And you hope he's jailed for the rest of his life. Mr Whiter-than-white wants him out of the way so that he doesn't have to be pleasant to someone who's been to jail."

"That's ridiculous."

"I'd rather be ridiculous than a pompous hypocrite."

"The police accept that I wasn't driving the car. They demand to know who was, but have agreed not to press me to tell them until tomorrow."

"And when you've told them, you'll drink champagne and every bubble will be a laugh."

"Even though it's my duty to tell them, I don't want—"

"God, when you say 'duty', you're Uriah Heep in the flesh!"

"I know he's your cousin, I know the two of you are very close—"

"You don't know a bloody thing."

He'd hoped to soften the impact of the news, but seemed to have provoked near hysteria. Glumly, he said: "The best thing is for me to ring Keith . . ."

"You're not going to gloat," she shouted. "I'll tell him how you're such a bastard, you're rushing to the police to say he had the car."

Her many bitter accusations hurt, even though he accepted that she was so shocked she was irrational.

Having watched Ryan leave to return to the office, Laura hurried up to their bedroom and phoned Tyler's office. Franchine, at her most refined, asked her to wait. When Tyler spoke, she interrupted him and said in a rush of words: "I'm scared. Alan's just been back home—"

"It's known as a pre-prandial quickie."

"For Christ's sake stop being smart. He came back because the police say they've found out his car was repainted by some crook and this means it did hit the old woman. He's telling the police tomorrow that you borrowed it. It's all nonsense, isn't it? You didn't have anything to do with the accident?"

"Haven't I told you that a dozen times? Listen, my nervous little kitten. The police are using the oldest trick in the book. They think someone borrowed his car, so they feed him a packet of lies designed to panic him and make him confess who it was. One thing's for sure. If he falls for that and tells them, they'll bang me up so quickly I won't have time to shout 'alleluia'. And they'll do their best to make certain the judge hands me the longest possible stretch."

"I can't think about it. We've got to stop him. How? Oh, God, how, when he'll never listen because now he thinks it's his duty to tell them?"

"There's usually a way of persuading even the blind to imagine they can see—" There was a long silence.

"Are you still there?" she asked.

"Thinking hard and coming up with an idea. Know the best way of persuading someone awkward to do something? Form a bond with him. So I'll agree that what he sees to be his duty, he must do, no matter what the consequences. Then I'll swear by Sir Galahad, who has to be his patron saint, that no matter what the police allege, I had no accident in his car. Humbly, I'll appeal for his help to prove my innocence. Unable to refuse such a request from someone who understands the true meaning of duty, he'll agree . . . Encourage him to talk with me this evening; override any objections he thinks up. Will you do that for me?"

"I'll do anything."

"We must put that to the test!"

Convinced that Laura's attitude towards him would be just as hostile as when he had left in the middle of the morning, perhaps even more so since time healed wounds, but enlarged resentments, Ryan decided not to return home for lunch. About to ring her to say that very important work had unexpectedly come into the office, he suddenly saw this white lie as cowardly and illogical – the more time that elapsed before he saw her again, the greater her resentment . . .

He did not expect the greeting he received on arriving home for lunch. She kissed him several times. She nibbled his neck as she said – words muffled: "I'm so sorry, my darling. I was so terribly beastly. Ever since you left, I've been wondering

159

how I could have said such terrible things. Can you possibly forgive?"

"All forgotten."

She stepped back. "I'm telling the world I have the most perfect husband."

"I trust the world is listening."

She waited until he'd hung up his overcoat – the temperature had risen little since daybreak – then linked her arm with his. "I was so frightened you'd be terribly angry that I had to do something to try and make you nicer. So I went out and bought some smoked salmon to have before the steaks and I've cooked your favourite pudding."

"Think me angry at least once a week."

It was while she was serving the maple syrup steam pudding that he said: "Keith phoned me just before I came back."

She lifted out a wedge of pudding and put it on a plate.

"He wants me to meet him this evening to talk things over even though I did what I could to make him understand there was nothing to discuss."

She passed him the plate. "Did you agree?"

"No. And then he kept on and on until I had to cut him short and ring off. He said he'll phone again. I wish he'd understand."

"Won't you—"

"Won't I what?"

"It doesn't matter."

"It obviously does. Tell me what you want."

"The police could be wrong, couldn't they?"

"The evidence now is very strong."

"But they could. You've always said that no one's omniscient. Suppose they are wrong. Think what that could mean to Keith. Listen to what he wants to tell you."

160

"I'm sorry, but I'm quite certain that nothing he can say will change anything."

"How can you say that before you hear him? . . . Please, please, for my sake. Then I'll know that everything possible's been done."

"All right. But don't build up your hopes."

"He swears he didn't hit anyone when he was driving your car."

He sadly wondered when she would finally accept the truth; and how much it would hurt when she did?

When he came to the cross-roads for the second time, Ryan decided that in this part of the county, the rolling English roads really had been made by a rolling English drunkard – and one with a penchant for mazes.

He turned left even though this would take him in the opposite direction to that which he judged he wanted to go, having turned right on the previous occasion. The lane, overhung by hedgerow trees, finally looped round to bring him to The Grand Old Duke which stood at the beginning of the village. Tyler had told him he'd chosen it because of the quality of the real ale it served; he didn't like ale, real or unreal.

The large car-park was mostly in deep shadow because it was ringed – unusually – by holly trees and there was only one wall bracket light. Two cars were already parked there and he drew up not far from one. He turned off lights and engine, raised the collar of his overcoat to counter the drizzle which had begun, but did not immediately climb out. This was not a meeting he would have accepted but for Laura and he was still uncertain how he should go about making it absolutely clear that nothing could alter his decision finally to tell the police the truth . . .

Jeffrey Ashford

He stepped out, shut the door and activated the central locking. He began to walk towards the side entrance of the pub.

"Mr Ryan?"

He stopped and turned to face two men who had just left the nearer car. He did not recognise either of them. "Yes?"

They moved with professional skill. A blow to the stomach doubled him up, a second blow to the back of his head blasted him into unconsciousness.

Twenty-Two

Laura was watching the television when the front door bell rang. She wondered if Alan had forgotten his keys? Even Homer nodded. She left the sitting-room and went through to the hall, stood within easy reach of the panic button in the wall to the left of the front door. "Is it you?"

"I can guarantee it's me."

"Keith!" She turned the lock, opened the door.

"God, what a night!" Tyler said as he entered. 'It's started to piss like a giraffe." Water dripped from his leather jacket on to the floor.

"Where's Alan – garaging the car?"

"Still at the pub. He met a couple of blokes he knows and said for me to come along and he'd follow when he could."

"Who were they?"

"Never clapped eyes on them before. Probably highly respectable since he didn't introduce me." He took off his jacket and hung it on the stand. "They're probably after free advice. He's such a soft touch."

"That's one thing you two have in common." His hands became busy.

She said, a shade breathlessly: "We'd better not."

"We'd better yes."

"But he mustn't catch us."

163

"He won't."

"He might."

"I'll bolt the doors and then you'll have time to dress."

"He'll wonder why I'd do that when he wasn't home."

"I'll tell him I've heard there's a homicidal maniac on the loose and decided I should have your interests in my hands."

"You're being impossible."

"Merely entertaining."

She moved her arm to look at her watch. "It's almost midnight." She sat up. "Where on earth is Alan?"

"Did you know your left tit is larger than your right one?"

"I'm worried."

"There's no call. It's not all that obvious."

"About Alan."

"He's fine."

"But he can't still be giving free advice. Something must have happened to him."

"I expect something has."

She stared down at him. "You sound almost as if you know what that something could be."

"And if I do?"

Her voice rose. "What are you saying?"

"For starters that I was driving the Astra when it hit the old woman."

"Oh, my God! No! You've told me again and again you don't know anything about the accident. You're trying to scare me."

"I needed you to sound absolutely convincing when you spoke to the police. You're a good liar as far as Alan's concerned, but he's so naïve that he probably believed you

164

when you told him you were a virgin. The police are in a different league."

"You . . . you aren't just frightening me?"

"That night, I had a meal with a business acquaintance and we cracked a couple of bottles. After we left the restaurant I drove a bit sharpish as we rounded a corner and there was the stupid old cow standing by the car. There was no way of missing her."

"If it was really her fault, why didn't you stop?"

"The last thing I wanted was for the police to breathalyse me and then become interested in the bloke I was with."

"Why did he matter? Who was he?"

"What you don't know, you don't have to worry about."

"But they know it was Alan's car and he's going to tell them you were driving it. They'll find out everything and because—"

"Because I've form, I'll be looking at a fifteen year stretch."

"No!" She gripped his arm.

"Unless—"

"What?"

"You're willing to play things my way."

"How can you ask? You know I will."

"Easy to say."

"I will."

"You'll tell the police your beloved husband has disappeared and you don't know where he is; that he was so worried before he vanished, you're frightened he must have done something terrible?"

"But he'll be here—"

"Not so."

"What . . . what are you saying now?"

"He was going to give the police my name so it became a question of self-preservation."

"What have you done?"

"Made certain that for a while he'll be keeping his news to himself."

"What's that mean?"

"There's no call for panic. He'll be leading a healthy life."

"Oh, God! Where is he?"

"Cruising around with a friend of mine."

"You . . . you can't do this."

"I've done it."

"But—"

"D'you want him to go to the police and tell them I had the car?"

"Of course not."

"You've a choice. Alan safe and sound, but not in a position to chat to the police. Me in jail, and good for nothing when I come out because a long stretch rots a man's mind as much as his body."

"Do you swear he'll be all right?"

"I promise that you'll never hear him speak one word of complaint about the way he's been treated." He reached up to pull her gently down. "Just think on this, my little passion flower. Life would be incredibly boring without me around to pluck your fruit."

Ryan returned to a formless world and was violently sick. Through thumping pain he heard, as if from an immense distance, someone's speaking, but the words were senseless. He opened his eyes, but all he could make out was a blurred gargoyle. Gratefully, he lost consciousness.

*　　*　　*

166

Meyer used the internal phone to speak to the front desk. "Is Mr Ryan there?"

"No, sir," replied the duty PC.

"Let me know the moment he arrives."

"Yes, sir." Only a very keen ear would have caught the inflection which expressed the weary annoyance at having been given the same order for the third time.

Meyer opened a file and read the top paper inside; he reached the bottom of the page and realised he'd not assimilated anything.

Lipman entered the office. "Is there any news of him?"

"Not yet."

"Does his wife or the office know where he is?"

Meyer didn't answer. He'd not done the obvious and made direct inquiries because for once he was unwilling to face facts. He did not want confirmation that he'd been taken for a fool.

"It's nearly half past."

"I know that as well as you do."

"He might have been caught up in some high-powered consultation with an important client; or, I suppose, he might just have forgotten."

Meyer, determined not to suffer any more subversive insolence, said: "Go and find out what's happened to him."

Lipman left the room. Meyer communed with himself. There were still a few in the world whom he was prepared to believe were essentially honourable and, despite everything, he believed Ryan to be one such. To be wrong would be to have his judgement proved hopeless, his faith absurd . . .

Lipman returned. "His office says he hasn't turned up and they've had no word from him. His wife told me that last night he was very worried, but he wouldn't tell her what was wrong other than that it was to do with having to come and see us

167

this morning. Then he said he had to go to a pub. When he left, he said goodbye in such a strange way that she became afraid and hardly slept all night. She's spent this morning wondering whether to get in touch with us ... It's clear he recognised he'd reached the end of the line and so he's done a runner."

"If he wasn't driving the car, at worst he's been guilty of trying to pervert the course of justice."

"That's a big 'if'."

"Not if you remember the second saloon car that was in the garage that night."

"Tillett's evidence is about as shaky as you can get."

"But that observation was made before Ryan had fed him the possibility that he'd been mistaken, so it's likely good. How would Ryan have known to take the car to Lister to have the work done?"

"He handles a fair number of criminal cases. The name could have cropped up and he remembered it. Surely the big question is, would someone in Ryan's position risk everything for a friend?"

"Friendships can be very deep."

"That deep?"

Hadn't he, in a different context, said that they had their limits?

"We'd better put out a general call for him before he can get too far."

"Not yet." Once that was done, everything would be on record. If one could summon up sufficient optimism, there was still time for Ryan to turn up with a valid explanation for his delay.

Because his mind seemed to have been swaddled in cotton wool, it took Ryan a long time to work out why the world was so unstable, but eventually he reasoned that he must be at sea. He lay on the bunk and stared up at the bulkhead, covered with pebbled insulation, the primitive air conditioning louvers, and the exposed pipes; he moved his head to look the length of the cabin and saw that a metal deadlight masked the port.

The cabin door opened and the gargoyle of his earlier confusion entered. She had wiry, chaotic, ginger hair, a flat forehead, bird's nest eyebrows, a nose which had been broken and badly reset, puffy cheeks that were veined with a patchwork of red and disfigured by moles from which grew long hairs, an overshot jaw, and it would have been kind to describe her body as shapeless. Only her eyes, dark brown and luminous, held beauty and they ironically emphasised her ugliness.

She stepped up to the bunk and spoke in what, after a while, he identified as Spanish. When she realised he could understand nothing, she struggled to speak a few words in English, but he could make no sense of them. Finally, she mimed the act of eating.

He shook his head. "Something to drink. Water."

That she could understand some English seemed clear when she went over to the wooden holder on the bulkhead to the side of the wash-basin, lifted out a decanter and glass, half filled the glass and carried this to the bunk.

He held the glass in a hand that trembled slightly, drank avidly. For a brief moment, he experienced pleasure, then he suffered a period of explosive vomiting that left him careless of where his vomit reached.

With astonishing strength, she lifted him off the bunk and on to the settee. She undressed him, despite his futile attempts to halt her, and used a hand towel to sponge him down, a second one to dry him.

169

She left the cabin, quickly returning with clean bedclothes with which she remade the bunk; she helped him up from the settee and on to the bunk. She picked up the badly soiled clothes and mimed the act of washing them, added a sheet and blanket to the bundle, crossed to the door.

"Thank you for being so kind," he said, instinctively observing the social niceties despite the bizarre situation in which he was.

Her hand on the door handle, she stared intently at him for several seconds, then left. It seemed to him that the expression in her brown eyes had been one of surprise and confusion . . . If anyone had the right to be confused, it was he. One moment in a logical world, the next in bedlam.

Twenty-Three

R yan awoke and mentally surveyed himself. His headache had eased and was now an irritation, but not much more, his left arm was stiff, his stomach was sore but, he was convinced, not in danger of further explosive action.

He found and switched on the bulkhead light and visually examined the cabin in far greater detail than before. It was oblong, some ten feet long and eight wide. Crammed within this space were the bunk, under which were drawers, a wash-basin, desk, cupboard, and settee; his clothes, neatly folded, lay on the settee and his shoes, newly polished, were on the deck.

The gentle movements of the ship almost lulled him back to sleep, but then she was caught out of rhythm and pitched more heavily, causing him to grab the wooden edge of the bunk to steady himself. For a while he held on, but released his grip as regularity returned. He climbed down on to the deck, dressed. As he moved around, he discovered that the deadlight had been spot-welded to the port which could not be raised and the door was locked. In effect, he was in a cell.

He slumped down on the settee and let his body sway to the ship's movements. The two men in the car-park of The Grand Old Duke had called on him to identify himself. How had they known he would be driving to that pub? Tyler, certain he was about to be identified to the police the

171

following morning, had employed violence and kidnapping to prevent its happening.

Ryan heard the click of the lock just before the door opened. A burly man with strong features and a luxuriant beard, wearing a shabby reefer jacket with four gold stripes on each shoulder and grey flannels, stepped inside. "Good to see you are looking better."

"Who are you?" he demanded.

"Captain Antonios Samaras." He reached across for the chair, set this between door and settee, sat. "I understand you were a very sick man." He smiled. "Doubly unfortunate when one has not had the pleasure of over-indulging beforehand."

Ryan was bewildered by the friendly manner. "What the hell's going on?"

"You are on board the SS *Rykonis* and—"

"Why am I a prisoner?"

"You're no more a prisoner than I, which is to say that we are both confined to the ship, but free within that confinement."

"Free? When I'm in a cell?"

"This is no cell."

"The window can't be opened."

"The deadlight was permanently secured for some long forgotten reason so it is true the port cannot be opened, but it's chance which finds you in this cabin and not one with a free deadlight and porthole."

"The door was locked."

"Because Maria's intelligence is no greater than her beauty and she completely misinterpreted my orders to leave it unlocked."

"If I'm not a prisoner, why am I here? Why was I attacked and dragged aboard this boat?"

"Remember, Mr Ryan, that channel ferries and submarines are boats, ships are ships. Even when so old that soon her hull plates will resemble Gruyère, the *Rykonis* remains a ship . . . It became necessary for you to disappear. However, I can assure you that, despite the circumstances, there is absolutely no call for you to be worried. The trip will be a longish one, since we can only make eight knots and that when the weather is fine, but eventually you will be free to return home."

"You have to be lying."

"Why do you think that?"

"If I return, Keith will be in even more serious trouble."

"You believe he wants you murdered and I am a willing party to that? I admit to having small regard for many laws – but in that I am with the majority – but I observe my own standards. Had Keith asked me to assist in your murder, I would have refused with a great deal of anger. But when he offered me a considerable sum of money for your passage, I saw no reason to refuse. And as to what happens when you return to England, by then he will be in a country which welcomes wealthy residents who appreciate the lack of extradition agreements."

"Where's all his money coming from?"

"I'm sure the firm for which he works will discover the answer in due course."

"What about you? Where are you going to be when I tell the police exactly what's happened?"

"You are clearly a naïve man."

"What's that supposed to mean?"

"That it clearly has not occurred to you that your question is a declaration of intent. And if you are going to denounce me to the police as soon as you have the chance . . ." He became silent.

Ryan experienced fear so sharp that he seemed to experience its taste.

Samaras suddenly laughed. "I apologise for my sense of humour which, being Greek, typically is laced with a taste of hemlock . . . Naturally, you will tell the police all that has happened to you. But this is the last trip for me since, although not an Onassis or Niarchos, I am not averse to risk taking in somewhat unorthodox circumstances – as you will have gathered – and I have managed to make enough money to return to my homeland as a man of some property. After unloading, we will be sailing to our next loading destination. On arrival there, you will be held by friends until I and my crew have disappeared, then you will be free to return home. Naturally you will speak to the police. They will then inform the Greek authorities that I am wanted for questioning. However, it is not difficult to buy a fresh identity if you know where to purchase it and so I shall be Captain Samaras no longer and there will be no chance of my being identified quickly; in Greece, something that does not happen quickly, does not happen."

"You'll never get away with it."

"We fly under the Liberian flag so that offences committed aboard come under that country's jurisdiction. Even a simple problem can be persuaded to become one of such unsurmountable complexity that it is never resolved."

In the present day, no one could be kidnapped and held captive for weeks without the most thorough investigation being carried out to identify and punish those who were guilty. Yet, Ryan realised, while such an assumption might be warranted in Britain, it was not in many other countries . . . "Where are we now?" he finally asked.

"We will soon be rounding Ushant."

"And after that?"

The Cost of Innocence

"We sail to Djarka, a small port in Algeria where we discharge." Samaras stood. "You are naturally at perfect liberty to go anywhere aboard that you wish, but I strongly advise you not to go down to the main deck. This company is run on cutthroat commercial lines and so the crew are drawn from The Lump, which is the name given to unemployed seamen in the eastern Mediterranean. Like all scum, they never lose the chance to abuse someone they can be certain is not one of their kind and not equipped to defend himself. They might well attack you for no better reason than that you have shaved. Equally, I suggest you normally eat here, in this cabin, rather than in the saloon, since my officers show no desire to imitate gentlemen and their table manners would undoubtedly astonish you. But from time to time, I should be grateful if you will join me in my cabin for a meal – it would be a pleasure to have an intelligent conversation." He turned to leave.

"Hang on."

He turned back.

"I'd like to let my wife know I'm all right."

"Naturally. I'll tell the wireless officer to send a cable for you which can be relayed to your wife by someone ashore – necessary to hide the fact you're at sea. I regret that I shall have to read it before transmission to make certain it gives nothing away. Do you have paper on which to write?"

"No."

"I'll tell María to bring you some and a pen. The circumstances being what they are, you'll probably like to make the message a long one – do so. Some economies need to be overlooked!" Samaras smiled, then left.

The ship altered course and picked up an altered rhythm of movement as the seas met her at a different angle, but Ryan failed to notice that fact. His previous fear was replaced by

175

perplexity and a growing sense of resentment. His world had always been one in which a person was largely responsible for his own destiny. Yet he had always observed honourable standards (if he had recently not kept strict honour with his principles, his motives had been honourable), but this attention to duty had not protected him . . .

The future cannot change the past, but the past can confuse the future. Regrets were not only useless, they were potentially harmful since he needed to accept the situation as it was, not as he would have it. He stood and immediately had to grab the edge of the basin for support. Once balanced, he stared at the door. Samaras had said that it had been locked through a mistake. The truth or a lie? The answer could be of vital significance to him. He crossed the deck and gripped the door handle, waited for the ship to return to an even keel, turned and pulled. The door opened . . .

He left the cabin to enter a cross-alley that led into a main alleyway running the length of the accommodation and went along this to come out on deck. He leaned on the rails and briefly looked down at the after deck, then out to sea. The wind was strong and when a wave broke, it picked up the spray and lashed it across the water. A low cross swell spoke of a distant storm. The sky was overcast, the clouds a dirty grey. Out on the beam was a supertanker, a shape lacking in detail because of distance and relatively poor visibility. He stared at her, his thoughts racing. If he could find something to signal with . . . Realism, returned. Even if he managed that, how would he signal, knowing no morse? How could anyone on her see him? . . . 'And in the face of hope denied, hope faded.'

He was becoming cold. He climbed the starboard ladder up to the boat deck, walked for'ard. There were signs of neglect everywhere. The teak decking had not been holystoned for so long that it was badly blotched; the starboard boats, davits, and crucifixes, were filthy, the rope falls grey with age; the deck house bulkhead had more rust than paint; the single, squat funnel was so blackened that the details of the house badge were obscured; an engine-room ventilator had partially collapsed and been left to rock to the ship's movements.

As he came level with the doorway into the captain's flat, Samaras stepped out. "You see – not a cell! And now you feel fit enough to pace the decks?"

"I needed the fresh air."

"That, the sea offers in abundance . . . Do you have the message that's to be sent to your wife?"

"I left the room before María could bring me paper and pen."

"Cabin, Mr Ryan . . . Had you rubbed two peseta coins together that would have brought her running immediately, or so I have been reliably informed."

"She's been very kind to me," Ryan said quickly.

"It is pleasant to hear someone defend her . . . Come into my cabin and write your message and I'll take it along to Sparks so that he can send it immediately and your wife has to suffer no further uncertainty."

He mumbled his thanks, conscious of the irony of thanking the other for making his captivity less mentally distressing. He followed into a short cross-alley and then through into a spacious smoke-room.

"As I'm sure you've realised," Samaras said, "the *Rykonis* was built a long time ago, when the captain had considerably more space than he needed and the crew considerably less than they did. These days, equality has been introduced which is bad for discipline since that relies on visible inequality . . . Sit down at the desk. You'll find paper and several ballpoint pens, one of which may work."

Ryan sat, picked put a sheet of paper from the lower right-hand cubby-hole, a pen out of the small opened drawer on the left. About to write 'My Darling', he checked his hand. This message would be read by Samaras, the wireless operator, and whoever relayed it in England, and he was embarrassed to know they would see the words, however normal they would be. He omitted them. She would understand and know they had been spoken in his mind . . . He emphasised that he was fit and well and would be back home before long; he asked her to speak to John Short at Amshot and Feakin and explain what was going on . . .

He stood. "I've finished."

"I'll take it along to Sparks right away, but first – I apologise very sincerely – I must read what you've written."

He handed over the sheet of paper. Samaras read, looked up: "As expected, totally discreet. One is very certain you are English."

A compliment or a criticism?

"Now, may I offer you coffee and a cake? Surprisingly, our baker is good at his job."

"No, thanks."

"Still a little under the weather? I prophesy that by to-morrow you will have found yourself a seaman's appetite."

Twenty-Four

Three days after Ryan's disappearance, Parker braked to a halt in front of the open gateway of Ragstone Hall. He stared at the dark green BMW in the right-hand garage. Is that interesting? he asked himself. Dunno, he answered, but that's some speed wagon!

He drove to the second gateway. He left the car, crossed the pavement, swung open the heavy metal door and went through to the garden in which a man was scarifying the lawn. To live in a place like this was really to live, he thought as he walked up the path, even if the neighbourhood was somewhat downmarket.

He climbed the steps into the grandiose portico, rang the bell. Laura opened the door. " 'Afternoon, Mrs Ryan," he said cheerfully. She might be a bitch, but she could surely make a man forget all his troubles when he returned home. "Sorry to bother you yet again, but have you heard anything?"

"Nothing. Had I heard, I'd have told you. Where is he?"

"I wish we knew."

"You should do. Something terrible has happened to him, hasn't it?"

"At the moment, there's no suggestion of that."

"You can think it's just normal for him to disappear?"

"No, of course not, but ... Mrs Ryan, if it'll help,

179

ninety-nine out of a hundred missing people eventually turn up alive and well."

"But the hundredth doesn't?"

Parker changed the conversation. "When I was driving past your garages, I noticed the BMW."

"Well?"

"Is it yours?"

"You know it isn't."

He waited.

She said tightly: "It belongs to my cousin. He's been kind enough to be with me at this terrible time."

"Glad to hear you've company; it always helps."

Back at the station, he reported to Meyer. "I called on Mrs Ryan on the way back."

"Has there been any contact?"

"She says not. But there is something—"

"Well?"

"There was a dark green BMW in the second garage. That had me remembering Tillett saying first off that he'd seen a dark coloured saloon in the garage when he met Ryan on the pavement on the twenty-second. I asked Mrs Ryan about it. She said it belonged to her cousin and he'd turned up to keep her company and help her cope. What was odd was how extra sharp she became after I mentioned the BMW; she almost bit her words in half."

"So what are you suggesting?"

"That maybe the BMW was the car Tillett actually did see. We reckon Ryan was covering for someone; his wife's cousin would fit the bill very nicely."

"A supposition based on an assumption."

"It could surely be worth a follow up?"

"If the cousin did borrow the Astra, we're not going to be

able to prove that with Tillett's evidence a shambles and the cousin denying it as hard as he can."

"A little deeper digging might turn up something fresh."

"More likely, the same old rotting rubbish."

"It was just a thought," Parker said defensively.

"When I was starting, I served with a DI who made it clear he expected his DCs to do everything but think – that caused too much grief."

Ryan circled the boat-deck for the seventh time. What had happened in the Crickshaw case? Had Crickshaw finally decided to see reason? Had the case been passed on to one of the other partners. Probably not yet. They'd be waiting for him to return because his prolonged absence would call for definite change and lawyers fought change all the way. And Laura? She would have been worried out of her wits by his disappearance, but his cable would have reassured her . . .

Ribald laughter from aft – audible because of a following wind – interrupted his thoughts. When this was repeated, he came to a stop, turned, and went to the rails. On the main deck, a group of seamen by the winch house at number four hatch were indulging in rough horse-play. The captain called the seamen a rabble and scum. Not words he would ever have used to describe anyone, but what he had seen of the crew suggested that probably they were not inappropriate . . .

The group churned round and one fell on to arms and legs and another reached down and pulled up the jersey, shirt and vest of the kneeling person to release two huge, shapeless breasts. As the men laughed, María looked up, her expression one of resigned despair.

Ryan, without thought, shouted: "What the hell are you doing?"

They stared at him. One of them said something that made

the others laugh; then he reached down and waggled one of Maria's breasts.

Ryan crossed to the starboard ladder and hurried down that, careless of the seaman's rule always to descend facing inboard, and down the second ladder to the main-deck. It was only as he came abeam of number four hatch coaming that he recalled the captain's advice to stay on top.

Maria was still on all fours.

The seaman, his untrimmed beard parted by a long scar, again waggled the enormous breast. "Very good. You want?"

"Leave her alone."

He contemptuously looked Ryan up and down, spat, reached behind his back and brought out a knife with a six inch blade. He jerked his thumb in the direction of the upper decks.

"Can't you get up?" Ryan asked Maria.

Her breasts swung as the ship pitched.

Watched by the others, the man with the knife came forward; he sliced the air in front of Ryan's nose. "Go. Quick."

Ryan had never before faced a brutally physical threat and his mind was flooded with the thought of the knife biting into his throat and slicing through artery and windpipe to leave him threshing out his life in fires of agony on the deck. Yet somehow he found the courage not to run, but to reach down to take hold of Maria under the armpits. As he struggled to help her to her feet, he felt the blade against his neck . . .

There was a bellowed order. The man hesitated, then lowered the knife.

Samaras came up to them, spoke rapidly and angrily. The onlookers moved away, but the man with the knife stood his ground and began to argue. Samaras moved with speed, grabbed his right arm and wrenched it back and round, forcing him to drop the knife; as the ship pitched more heavily than she had been, he was caught off balance and fell. There was sycophantic laughter from the onlookers. Samaras picked up the knife and hurled it over the side.

"Up top," he ordered Ryan.

"What about her—"

"Get up top," he shouted angrily.

Ryan made his way up and along to his cabin. As he sat on the settee, his hands began to shake. He recalled the feel of the blade on his neck and felt sick as imagination, ironically with an even greater sense of happening, again made him feel the metal slicing into his flesh . . .

Samaras entered. "Are you always such a bloody fool?"

Ryan looked up. "I had to do something. They were abusing her."

"How do you suppose she has survived? By allowing herself to be abused . . . You are on a rusty old tramp, crewed by a rabble from many countries, told to keep out of their way. Yet merely because they amuse themselves with a worn-out bag, you interfere with their fun. Is that because you are an English gentleman?"

"Perhaps."

"Then it is small wonder there are so few of your kind left."

"You're suggesting I should have left her to their tender mercies?"

"She would have survived. You might not have."

"I can't believe they would actually have killed me."

"Actually. Is that what you would have said in a refined accent as Vassilios actually cut your throat?"

"Just because I tried to help her?"

"You know nothing. But perhaps an English gentleman must know nothing about such people or he is no longer a gentleman . . . Do not go down to the main-deck again, not if you see them raping a couple of mermaids." He left.

After a while, Ryan picked up the paperback copy of *Barchester Towers*. He had expected Samaras's literary tastes to reach no higher than thrillers, but every book in his small library was entitled to be called a classic; Ryan liked to think of himself as possessing an educated mind, but there were many of the titles which he had not read. He pondered the complex character of Samaras. A man with the power of command, little or no fear, ready to face a potential killer to save someone he clearly viewed with a degree of amused contempt; but apparently unable to understand how anyone should bother to help a woman who had fallen as low as Maria, holding on his ship a victim of kidnapping . . .

He began to read, but could not concentrate on the story which suddenly seemed of such small consequence when placed against the feel of a blade and a woman who had experienced depths that Mrs Proudie had never imagined.

There was a knock on the door and he opened it. As usual, he took the tray from Maria and put it down on the settee. "How are you?" he asked. "Did they hurt you?"

She spoke in Spanish, trying so hard to make him understand her meaning that she brought her face close to his, as if propinquity would help comprehension. He caught a scent that hinted at clogged drains.

Moving too quickly for him to begin to guess what she intended, she grabbed his right hand and kissed it with fervour many times.

"Don't do that. There's no call for it," he said, embarrassed by such emotional thanks.

She released his hand and left.

He sat on the chair, reached across for the tray and set this on his lap. The meat was tough, the greens a soggy mess, the potatoes floury. The jam roly-poly looked as if it had been boiled in soiled rags. Despite this, and all that had happened, he ate quickly. Samaras had said that he would soon gain a seaman's appetite.

Twenty-Five

M eyer parked to the side of the main building at county
HQ, six floors of pseudo-Georgian architecture. He got
out of the car and hastily pulled on his overcoat even though
he was not far from the side entrance; since daybreak, the
wind had contained icicles. He looked up at the sickly grey
sky and with Irish logic thought that if it rained, it would
snow. The return journey to Amplestone on snow-covered
roads, surrounded by lunatic drivers who saw no reason to
decrease speed despite such conditions, would be a fitting
finale to the forthcoming meeting with the detective chief
superintendent.

He took the lift to the third floor and walked along the
main corridor to the secretary's room. She asked him to wait
as Superintendent Potter was in conference with the assistant
chief constable. He sat and morosely wondered how much
more time he was going to have to waste?

Twenty minutes passed before Potter – rapidly becoming
a butterball of a man – entered. "I'll need some letters done
later on, Doris . . . 'Morning, Bill. And a bloody cold one!
Come along in."

Potter, Meyer thought sardonically, had so developed his
hail-fellow-well-met persona that he sometimes forgot to drop
it when addressing his juniors.

They settled in a large room, through the single window

of which could be seen playing fields and, just visible beyond them, the skid pan used in advanced driving instruction.

Potter shuffled through several files on the desk, found the one he wanted, opened it, and brought out a sheet of paper which he read through half-moon glasses "Your clear-up rate's not looking too bright, is it?"

"Not for the past month."

"And the month before and the one before that weren't any better. I've had the ACC asking me if E division's rate is going into free fall."

"I hope you pointed out, sir, that—"

"Every crime not cleared up is a defeat; a defeat for us and a defeat for law and order—"

Meyer listened to words he'd heard before. Potter, sometimes called to appear on TV to comment on criminal matters, had clearly begun to consider himself an orator.

". . . Well, that's the situation. So you'll go back and kick arse and soon I'll be able to tell the ACC that those percentage points are rising instead of falling."

"Given our share of luck," Meyer said, knowing the phrase would irritate.

"Luck has no relevance. I expect my DIs to appreciate that luck belongs on the race track. Do you understand?"

"Yes, sir."

Potter picked out a second sheet of paper from the file and read this. "What progress have you made tracing Ryan?"

"The wife's heard nothing from her husband and there's no worthwhile sighting reported, so we've no idea where he is."

"No trace of the car?"

"None."

"Presumably, he drove across to the Continent, instead of to the pub?"

"It's the most likely scenario since we can be virtually certain he never entered The Grand Old Duke. I've tried to track him through the ferry companies and Eurotunnel, but their records aren't up to that."

"It's very unfortunate that he managed to skip after you'd finally amassed sufficient evidence to arrest him."

"It was my judgement that there was more to be gained by playing it long."

"And that's why you agreed he could turn up at the station the next day without any security that he'd do so other than his word? You accepted his word like some newly joined recruit who doesn't yet know his arse from his elbow?"

There was only one way in which Potter could have learned that – through someone in E division. Meyer didn't hesitate in mentally naming Lipman.

"Well?"

"I did agree to him coming to the station the following morning, but—" Meyer did his best to obscure the facts.

To match Meyer's mood when he left the building, there should have been a blizzard raging, but the sullen clouds were still threatening rather than delivering. He settled behind the wheel of his car, started the engine, drove out on to the road and cut through the back streets to pick up the motorway at the first junction.

He settled in the middle lane behind a coach. Lipman must have a direct line through to the detective chief superintendent, so it would be a mistake openly to go gunning for him since such a move might well backfire. But there were other, subtle, ways in which to make his life miserable . . .

He'd done himself no favours by accepting Ryan's promise, Meyer thought bitterly. Potter would make certain his name did not figure in the next promotion list. He wondered how

189

in the hell he could have so misjudged as to believe Ryan would keep his word? Were the cynics right when they said there was no room for honour in a beefburger world?

Ryan stood for'ard of the captain's flat and watched the *Rykonis* edge towards the quay, unaided by tugs. He knew nothing about ship handling, yet was certain that Samaras was exhibiting great skill. Why did a man who so clearly possessed the power and skills of command not captain a modern ship instead of a tired old rust-bucket? Because of a reason, or reasons, unconnected with his professional abilities? Surely there was evidence of that in the fact he had agreed to have on board a man he knew to have been kidnapped . . .

Heaving lines were thrown, hawsers and wire backsprings run ashore and then tightened by windlass and winches to bring the hull hard up against huge cane fenders. Ryan could just hear the jangle of bells from the bridge as 'Finished with Engines' was rung on the telegraphs. The ship's gangway, rigged with loose hand ropes, was lowered; once in position, the ropes were tightened. Samaras went ashore.

Ryan decided it would be difficult to find a more desolate spot. The single crane looked as if it had not worked in years, the cargo sheds were in a state of disrepair; beyond the sheds was a collection of hovels, beyond them only scrubland backed by bleak hills.

Warmed by the sun, even though it was only the beginning of March, he watched the unloading at number three hold get under way. Port and starboard derricks were raised and rigged in tandem, the inboard one above the middle of the hold, the outboard one above the quay, their runners coupled together. Tarpaulins had been removed, now the hatch boards were lifted by hand and the beams by the derrick. Dockers, looking like a gang of underfed cutthroats, went below by way of the boobytrap and soon the first crate was lifted by the inboard derrick and then, as the runner was slacked away and the outboard derrick took the strain, positioned above the quay before being lowered. The shore gangs, using ancient hand trolleys that made the task an onerous one, pushed the crate into the nearest shed.

It seemed inexplicable that cargo should be discharged in so isolated and moribund a port, lacking any means of rail trans-shipment. Probably this was further evidence that the European Union's economists were alive and well.

On the ninth day in port, he returned to his cabin to find a copy of the *Daily Telegraph* on the settee, its condition suggesting it had been scrumpled up and thrown away, to be rescued by someone who had carefully smoothed it out. That someone was surely María? But who had brought a three day old *Telegraph* to Djarka?

He switched on the bulkhead light, sat and read, abruptly made aware of the outside world. By page four, he began to think that ignorance truly was bliss since almost every column exposed man's inhumanity to man. Page five gave him cause for more immediate and personal concern. Under the heading, 'Solicitor Still Missing', he read that Alan Ryan, a senior partner in the firm of Amshot and Feakin. solicitors in Amplestone, was still missing after having disappeared more than two weeks before. He had last been seen when he left home in his car on the seventeenth of February, intending, according to his wife, to meet someone at The Grand Old Duke, a public house; since then, she had had no word from him. The police were conducting inquiries, but the lack of any evidence regarding his movements after leaving home meant that they had no idea where he currently was or whether he had suffered an accident. His car was also missing.

He dropped the paper, stared unseeingly at the bulkhead. Soon after they'd sailed, Samaras had promised the cable would be sent to Laura to assure her he was OK. Obviously, no cable had arrived. Samaras had forgotten the promise, decided it was not worth the effort of implementing, or lied.

Ryan left the cabin and made his way up to the captain's flat. Only the tiger was there, a thin, dehydrated man with a slightly curved spine, whose sallow, pinched face spoke of chronic ill health. In fractured English, he said the captain was ashore.

Ryan went out on to the boat-deck and paced this as he tried to assess the implications of what he had just discovered. If Samaras had forgotten or not bothered, then the only consequence was that Laura's worry and fear had been needlessly prolonged; if he had lied, then probably the motive had been to keep his prisoner's mind at rest . . .

As he approached the after rails, a burst of shouting caused him to come to a stop. The hatchman at number four was leaning over the coaming and rowing with those below. When he finally straightened up, he motioned with his right hand to the inboard winchman to resume lifting. There was a crackling sound from the runner and the derrick seemed to be vibrating, suggesting the weight of the hoist was testing its breaking strain. A very large crate came into sight as it reached the level of the upper 'tween deck; oblong, it only just cleared the hatchway. Ryan watched it swing very slowly across the deck and then drop down on to two trolleys. It was only then, as several men clustered around each trolley, that he noted the shipping marks on the side of the crate; these included the name 'Jeddah'. Why would cargo destined for Jeddah be unloaded in Djarka? . . . He turned as he heard someone approaching him.

Samaras came to a halt and the light wind fiddled with

his hair and beard. "My tiger said you were looking for me?"

"Yes."

"Then come along to my cabin and enjoy a drink as you tell me why."

They went into the captain's flat. Samaras asked Ryan what he would like, indicated the nearer arm-chair, secured to the deck, crossed to the cupboard in which he kept both glasses and bottles. "How can I help you?"

"You promised me you'd have a cable sent to my wife."

"Indeed."

"Was it sent?"

"Of course."

"She can't have received it because she still has no idea whether I'm still alive."

Samaras crossed to hand Ryan a drink, sat on the second arm-chair. "How would you know that?"

"The *Daily Telegraph* dated the fourteenth carries the report that I'm still missing and the police have no idea where I am or even if I'm still alive."

"There is someone here who sells English papers?"

"I found it."

"Where?"

About to answer, Ryan checked the words. The truth might harm María. "On the boat deck."

"How do you think it reached there?"

"Obviously it was discarded by someone who's arrived from the UK in the past three days."

"You know of such a person?"

"No."

"And neither do I."

There was a silence which Ryan broke. "Why didn't you send the cable as you said you would?"

"For a lawyer, you are eager to jump to conclusions."

"As a lawyer, I concentrate on facts."

"These are the facts. I told Sparks to send the cable and watched him while he did so. But as you were told, it did not go straight to your wife, but to a friend who was asked to phone it through to her. If she has received no such phone call, it is obvious I should have remembered that friendship calls for more hope than trust. I shall naturally make amends for my friend's incompetence. As soon as we are back at sea, a cable will be sent to someone else who will phone the message."

"Why should he prove any more reliable?"

"He is not a friend and he owes me money."

"To make absolutely certain, will you let me go ashore and phone her?"

"Out of the question."

"You have my word I will say nothing that can possibly indicate where I am."

"You are now in a world where a man's word changes character as required."

"All right, you do the talking. That will make certain she learns nothing except I'm alive."

"Phone calls can be traced."

"Your friend was going to phone in England."

"Having taken every necessary precaution."

"No one's going to be expecting the call so no one will have arranged to track it."

"The risk is too great."

"No cable was ever sent, was it? You're making certain my wife doesn't know I'm still alive."

"An absurd accusation."

"Is it? I've just watched a very large crate being unloaded."

"Can there be any connection between that fact and the message?"

"It was consigned to Jeddah. Is all the rest of the cargo for there?"

"Some is for Muscat."

"And that's being unloaded here?"

Samaras stood, went over to the bulkhead and pressed a bell. "Like all sailors, I'm inclined to be superstitious and your ability to find an English newspaper in this Godforsaken spot has me worried. You will be locked in your cabin until we are back at sea. Then you will need supernatural powers to leave us and I cannot believe someone so naïvely ready to expose his thoughts can possess them."

A seaman entered the cabin. Samaras spoke rapidly in Greek, turned to Ryan. "Please go quietly. It will be so much more pleasant for you."

Twenty-Six

I t was humiliating to discover how readily he had accepted
when he should have questioned, believed when he should
have doubted, trusted when he should have mistrusted. But
he had always lived in an ordered world and so, despite his
criminal work, it simply had never occurred to him that this
was a privilege; disorder was more natural than order.

The past was not yet an open book, but he could read
some of the pages. Tyler and Samaras – and others – had
organised a very large insurance swindle. Since the success
of their plan rested on there being no cause for suspicion –
insurance adjusters were so notoriously suspicious that even a
saint's statement of loss would require corroboration – it had
been essential that authority should never have the slightest
reason to learn of, or even suspect, a working relationship
between them since he was an ex-convict and Samaras had
to have an equally incriminating past or with all his skills
he would have held a good command. When the Astra had
hit Mrs Yates, their relationship had been threatened with
immediate exposure.

Tyler had called on Laura for help, certain that her
affection for him – brother more than cousin – was so
strong that she would accept his declaration of innocence
even in the face of apparently incriminating evidence.
Laura had set out to make him – her husband – betray

Jeffrey Ashford

himself in order to prevent the police's uncovering the truth . . .

There had been alarms for the conspirators, but after these had been overcome, it had seemed they'd won through. Then Lister had been arrested and proved the truth of the old saying, 'Never trust a man who offers you his trust'. Faced with imminent exposure, Tyler had decided there was only one way of avoiding catastrophe and that was, remove the source of danger. A task made easy by the victim's naïvety . . .

A captive held on land always posed a danger because he might escape or be rescued A captive held at sea could not escape and the chances of his being located, let alone rescued, were too small to worry about.

Samaras had played his part to perfection – the good natured rogue, ready to make a dishonest penny provided his doing so didn't really harm anyone, eager to make a captive's life as pleasant as was reasonable. But for the crate and the copy of the *Daily Telegraph*, his mask would not have dropped . . .

Cargo consigned to Jeddah and Muscat, unloaded in a port whose only asset was isolation, suggested that after discharging her cargo, the *Rykonis* would sail into the eastern Mediterranean to be scuttled. The insurance claim would be for cargo and ship . . .

The cabin door opened, startling him. María entered, a tray in her hands. Beyond her, standing in the cross-alley, was a burly seaman. She put the tray down on the settee, straightened up, and tried to speak in English, but yet again failed to say anything that made sense. In her frustration, she switched to Spanish. The seaman shouted, but when she continued to speak, he came into the cabin, gripped her shoulder and jerked her back so brutally that she cried out in pain.

"Leave her alone," Ryan said, as he came to his feet.

The seaman spun her to one side and into the bulkhead, took a step forward and hit Ryan in the stomach. Ryan collapsed to the deck. He heard her cry out again, but the stabbing agony left him indifferent to anyone else's plight.

Time eased the pain and finally he was able to haul himself up on to the chair. Dully, he accepted that all the pages could now be read. Realistically, there had never been any room for doubt as to what was printed on them. From the beginning, it had been decreed that he would go down with the ship. It had, perhaps, tickled Samaras's Greek sense of humour to explain to his captive how he would eventually be returned to the UK alive and well, knowing he was being actually believed.

Meyer looked across his desk as Parker entered.

"Greg said you were shouting for me?" Parker came to a halt.

"I've been waiting all day for your report on the Pearson case."

"It took an age to flush Feakin and even longer to persuade him to chat away."

"What did he have to say?"

"Nothing useful."

"Do you think that one day you could come in here and tell me something worth the effort?"

"Funnily enough, Guv, I reckon that that's what maybe I'm about to do. I called in on Mrs Ryan to hear the latest news, but before going in, I had a look at the garages and the BMW was there again. And when she opened the door and I said good morning—"

"Don't forget to tell me how many bloody times you blew your nose."

"The thing is, she was all polite and friendly and you

know what sort of a bitch she is. Added to which, she had that look."

"What the hell are you talking about?"

"The cat that's just finished a saucer of cream a minute ago."

"I have a DC comes in here and talks about cats and saucers of cream? What's next on the menu?"

"What I'm getting at is, she'd just been up on cloud nine. I'm convinced she and that cousin of hers had been playing bedroom poker."

"Has anyone ever told you you have a sewer for a mind?"

"Look at it this way. Ryan's a fair bit older than her and no great ball of fire. Along comes someone she calls cousin so as they can make sweet music together and hubby isn't suspicious. So when cousin borrows Ryan's car and smashes into the old woman because he's pissed, he says to the wife, I need your help, my darling; persuade your old man to cover for me. She's got her husband twisted round her little finger, or something, and even if it goes against the grain because he's so upright that a ruler looks crooked alongside him, he agrees. Then we have enough evidence to put the screws on him and he finally has the wit to realise that his only bet is to come clean. He tells us that's what he'll do the next day – after he's had a cuddle with the wife and made her understand why he's going to have to do what he is. She panics because she's going to lose all her happy-slappy days if cousin's inside and tells cousin what's afoot. He sees himself in the dock listening to a long stretch coming his way unless he does something real fast. So he lures Ryan to that pub, grabs him on arrival, and bundles him off to somewhere safe . . . What do you think?"

"You should find yourself a literary agent."

"It could be things have worked like that," Parker said defensively.

"Ryan could have made himself invisible, but I reckon it's unlikely."

"Surely it's worth following up the possibility?"

"You want me to spend more time on a case that's gone cold enough to freeze a penguin just because you enjoy dirty thoughts?"

"A woman doesn't look like she did unless her world's been moving so hard she still hasn't got her balance back."

"She was probably wondering if she'd ordered enough milk."

The plan had been simple in principle, very complicated to organise because there had to be no suspicion of fraud. The prime necessity was for the two ships to be in position as if by sheer chance. This meant each must load and sail within the normal terms of commercial maritime practice or, to put it in another way, each must complete loading – one in Europe, one in India – exactly on time and not be forced to leave behind cargo since tramps normally never turned up the chance of carrying even a couple of crates. Further, the *Stellar* must have aboard the kind of flotsam normally found after a ship sank, some of which would be readily indentifiable as having come from the *Rykonis*.

The MV *Stellar*, owned by a company registered in Panama, would sail from Bombay and steam through the Suez Canal at a speed which would bring her to the first predetermined point at the predetermined time of night. There, she would transmit a Mayday call in the name of the *Rykonis* (which would have been there had she not altered course immediately after dark), reporting a violent explosion and very serious fire in the engine-room. Two more, ever more urgent transmissions

201

would be made, to the effect that the fire was out of control, the explosion had blown a hole in the hull and the ship was settling quickly. Oil (as used by the *Rykonis* so that should analyses be made, they would confirm the source) would be discharged and the flotsam would be thrown overboard. The *Stellar* would sail on, to rendezvous with the *Rykonis* a few hours later.

Just as traces had to be left at the supposed position of the sinking, so none must be where the *Rykonis* actually went down. The four lifeboats would be broken up until the pieces could be dropped down a hatch; all lifebelts and lifebuoys would be locked into cabins with ports tightly clamped shut; everything that floated or conceivably might, would be stowed where there could be no chance of its breaking free.

Charges set against the hull in numbers two and four middle 'tween decks – low enough to ensure a heavy inrush of water, high enough to avoid the possibility of the double bottom being ruptured and releasing oil – would be exploded before the crew took to the boats from the *Stellar*.

The *Rykonis* would be posted as missing with all hands. And lacking the slightest proof of fraud, in due course the insurers would have to pay up.

Twenty-Seven

When, three days out from port, María brought lunch, she alerted Ryan to the fact that the end of the voyage was close, not by anything she said or did, but by that indefinable form of communication there could occasionally be between two people when emotions were running high.

He stared at the door after she had left and the seaman had locked it. When a man knew he was to be hanged in a fortnight, it concentrated his mind wonderfully; when he was certain he was to die long before that, it panicked his mind completely. Would they show him sufficient mercy to kill him before they left the ship; would they simply leave him locked in the cabin to drown? He'd once read that drowning was one of the less unpleasant forms of death, but that had to be the opinion of someone who couldn't be certain. To imagine holding one's breath until that was no longer possible; one's lungs filling with water that brought the white hot agony of suffocation . . . In truth, cowards did die many times before their deaths. History told of men who faced death without flinching. He must try to do that so that he could die with self-respect intact . . . He suddenly laughed, genuinely – if very temporarily – amused by the absurd image of himself as some Victorian hero, in a far distant corner of the globe, squaring his shoulders for the sake of an image that could not be recorded even in his own mind.

*　　*　　*

When María brought him supper, she looked at the lunch tray and the untouched food, then intently at him. She spoke Spanish so rapidly that it sounded like one endless word.

The seaman moved into the cabin doorway and angrily gave an order in Greek. She ignored him and put the one tray down on the settee, picked up the other, stared once again at Ryan so that he became convinced she was trying to transmit her thoughts . . .

The ship moved unexpectedly and she was caught off balance and allowed the tray in her hands to tilt; the plate of tinned peaches fell to the deck and shattered. She put the tray down on the deck, knelt, and began to scoop up the mess with the spoon. The seaman shouted at her and then raised his right foot and pushed her sideways so that she fell on to the patch of peach juice. His humour restored, he made no further effort to stop her.

She picked up the tray and stood. She faced Ryan and this time struggled to speak English, but the only word that had any possible meaning for him was 'eat' and he was far from certain that that was what she had been trying to say.

The seaman, no longer amused, ordered her out and after a final, prolonged look at Ryan, she left. The door was locked.

He wondered what María had so desperately been trying to tell him? Had she been making an emotional farewell? Tradition had it that the condemned man was offered choice for his last meal; his choice would not have been the glutinous mixture that faced him and his instinct was to leave it, as he had left lunch. But, perhaps absurdly, he decided that if she had been so concerned, he should at least make an effort to eat something.

He set the tray on his lap and trawled his fork through the

stew to discover if there were any pieces of meat that might be edible. Almost immediately the fork came into contact with something hard. He applied more pressure and brought to the surface an object which he failed to recognise until much of the gunge had slithered off it. He stared at the key and wondered at what risk to herself had she found and smuggled this to him? No wonder she had been so desperate to encourage him to eat . . .

Hope vanished almost as quickly as it had arrived. How could he escape? If he appeared before the crew had taken to the boats, they'd return him to the cabin – without the key; if after, how did he get safely away from the sinking ship? Hope returned. He'd find some way of saving himself, now that he'd been given the means to start doing so. He ate, his mind so concentrated on the future that he failed to judge that the stew was almost as unappetising as it looked.

His watch told him it was a quarter to twelve when he became aware of change; the background hum, which had persisted all the time they were at sea, was stilled. The engines had been stopped? The ship's movements changed and eased to confirm that this was so.

How soon would it be safe to leave the cabin? Was there any way of judging? Would they, before they abandoned ship, check he had remained locked in the cabin? Why should they, when they had every reason to believe it impossible for him to leave it?

He mentally tried to follow them, even while acknowledging this to be futile since there were no certainties with which to form a basis for judgement. As the minutes passed, time for him shortened as he suffered an ever increasing tension . . .

There was a muffled explosion and the ship shuddered; there was a second one. Unwittingly, they had given him the basis he had lacked. They would be abandoning ship now.

He crossed to the door and found the key would not go very far into the lock. In his panic, he cursed María for giving him the wrong key ... He forced himself to regain self-control, bent down and looked into the key-hole, could see nothing, which surely meant that the other key, inserted from the outside, was still in place. He had one more chance. He inserted the key again and pushed very hard. Abruptly, it surged forward. The gods were with him! The outside key had been lined up with the opening in the lock case. He unlocked the door, pulled it open, listened. The ship, being riveted, creaked gently to each lazy roll, but those were the only sounds.

He stepped into the cross-alley and as he did so, all the lights went out. Because the incoming waters had reached the dynamos? If so, there could be only little time left. Using a hand on the bulkhead as a guide, he moved along to the alleyway. The distance to the deck outside was shorter aft than for'ard so he turned left. A couple of minutes later, he stepped out of the accommodation.

The moon was almost full and there were few clouds in the sky so that visibility was good. To starboard, another ship was standing by and for a moment he was afraid of being sighted, then realised this was ridiculous; just as he could make out few details about her, so anyone aboard would be able to pick out few details on the *Rykonis* ... A lifeboat under power came into sight as it made its way towards the other vessel; on deck, the sea appeared almost calm, but the boat was pitching and occasionally the moonlight picked out spray around the bows.

Since the *Rykonis* had been abandoned, he ceased to worry and walked openly towards the corner of the accommodation; as he reached it, a seaman came round from for'ard.

He made no deliberate assessment of the situation; he did not logically work out that he must have a brief moment of advantage since he knew the seaman was an enemy, the seaman must initially believe him to be a fellow crew member; he did not consciously decide to seize that advantage by overcoming a lifelong hatred of violence; he just acted. He closed and brought his knee up as violently as he could. The seaman dropped to the deck, gagging, hands clasped to his groin.

From for'ard there came a shout which sounded like a name being called. Another seaman, having completed the final check, calling on his companion to leave? Already, the man at Ryan's feet was making less noise and it was clear that very soon he would have recovered sufficiently to call for help. The two of them would hunt him down and kill him before they finally left the ship; or if there were not enough time to risk gaining their revenge, they'd watch from a lifeboat to make certain he did not survive the sinking.

He had only one way of prolonging any chance of escape, yet even in the face of that certainty, he hesitated until there was a second call, which came from closer. The seaman opened his mouth; Ryan kicked him in the face and the bubbling moan of pain was proof of the injury he caused. He dragged the writhing seaman over to the rails and then, finding a strength he would not have thought he possessed, hauled him up and over. The seaman slid down the hull and splashed into the sea. Ryan, mentally numbed, stared at the body as it very slowly drifted away . . .

There was a third call, close enough to make it obvious that the oncoming man would soon round the corner. Ryan retreated into the accommodation and pulled the door shut. As he waited, terror seemed to squeeze his lungs. He thought he heard footsteps passing. Then a fourth shout, now only dimly heard, suggested the seaman had indeed gone past the door ... with the immediate danger past, Ryan found himself absurdly trying to believe that the man in the sea had recovered sufficiently to swim round the stern and be seen by his companions ...

Time passed. He opened the door and could hear only the sounds of the sea and the ship. He stepped out on deck and made his way to the port ladder to climb up to the boat deck.

All the lifeboats had gone and the threefold blocks swung freely. Even though he would not have known what to do if a lifeboat had remained, their absence panicked him. He hurried for'ard to where two lifebuoys with coiled lines attached had hung on the engine-room housing, but they were no longer there. His panic increased. He climbed the ladder to the wheelhouse and searched for something that would offer him hope of escaping the sinking ship without knowing what that something could be. Out on the wing, he saw that the other vessel was now stern on; she was sailing away, whoever was in command either careless or ignorant of the fact that one man was missing.

When he looked over the for'ard dodger, it was clear that very soon the sea would be sweeping over the foredeck. Once that happened, there could be little time left. María had given him the means of escaping from the cabin, but not of escaping the ship. Despair, or the refusal to despair – impossible to say which – suddenly triggered his memory. When he'd been free to walk the boat-deck, he'd noticed that on either side of the deck-housing was a steel locker, some eight foot long, on which had been painted by someone who was no sign writer, the single word 'Raft'. Would the lockers prove to be as empty as the davits?

He raced down the ladder and along the deck. Despite the moonlight, it was difficult to make out how the lid of the starboard locker was secured and initially he believed that it must be locked; common sense returned and he realised this had to be nonsense. A calmer examination showed that for some inexplicable reason the lid was hinged on the outboard side and opened from inboard once the two holding clamps were released. Inside, was an oblong of tightly packed, orange coloured rubber coated material, secured by quick release lashings (still there, unbeknown to him, because it did not bear the name *Rykonis* and secure in the locker there could be no chance of its floating).

The raft was far heavier than he had expected and by the time he had managed to extract it, he was breathless and sweating despite the coldness of the night. As he finally manoeuvred it clear of the locker, there was a drawn out metallic noise from somewhere aft – one of the bulkheads giving way as the pressure of the water increased?

Despite the need for speed, he paused – how did he get the raft into the water, how did he inflate it? When he looked across the deck at the empty davits, he realised that there was a clear run to the side of the ship; when he released the lashings, the material partially splayed out and instructions, written in black lettering so large that they could be read in the moonlight, told him to pull pin to inflate and an arrow directed him to two gas bottles, secured together. He released both pins and the raft inflated rapidly to the accompaniment of an angry hissing noise. Oval in shape, the sides were the buoyancy chambers; both the bottom and the loose cover that was attached to the sides were made of several layers of rubber coated material.

Having dragged the raft across the deck and between the davits, he was about to secure the end of the painter when a hint of seamanship made him realise that if he did this, he would not be able to release the painter when in the raft. He took it round the after davit and back, made it fast.

He pushed the raft across the scuppers and over the side. It fell a few feet, then checked and swung inboard as the ship sluggishly rolled. He experienced fresh fear as he imagined a sharp surface slicing into the raft and releasing the pressure . . . The ship rolled back to starboard, the raft was freed to fall to the water and drift aft until checked by the painter.

He went down the ladders to the main deck, where the sea was now swirling inboard as far as the hatch coaming at number four. From below came sounds of destruction. He crossed to the rails. The painter, arching from up top, was well out of reach. He climbed the rails and slid into the sea.

He was a strong swimmer, yet the few feet to the raft became a seemingly unbridgeable distance because stupidly he had removed neither shoes nor any clothes and sea and swell were much heavier than they'd appeared to be, even from the main deck. He could feel the strength draining away so quickly that he became convinced he would never make the raft. A swell swept him forward, the gap closed, and with a desperate lunge, he was able to grab one of the lifelines looped along the side.

It was a further struggle to drag himself aboard the raft, but eventually he managed this. With fingers that had become so chilled there was great difficulty in making them do what he wanted, he undid the painter. Very slowly, as the raft drifted away from the ship, it paid out until the end rose up, then whipped around the davit and fell back to the sea.

He looked through the opening in the cover and watched the *Rykonis*. Minutes passed, then suddenly her bows began to rise as her stern dipped under the water until she

was almost on end. She hesitated, then slid under with
smooth speed.

Despite the March sun, which was warm, and a sea that was
calmer so that there was no spray, it was not until well into
the morning before he began to dry; by the afternoon, he
ceased to feel as if even his bones had been frozen.

'Alone on a wide wide sea!" The empty loneliness crushed
the soul. What chance could there be that he would be sighted
in a limitless sea?

An easterly wind grew stronger and clouds began to obscure
the sun and the temperature dropped sharply, the sea began
to rise, waves slapped against the raft and he was forced
to close the two flaps in the cover and cower in what was
a claustrophobically small space. Never mind the pain of
thirst, how rough a sea could the raft survive?

By daybreak next morning, he was bitterly cold, suffering
from seasickness because the raft's motion was so different
from any he had previously experienced, his throat was aching
piercingly, and he knew extremes of both despair and hope
– one moment he was convinced he was already dying, the
next he found the inner resolution to believe that he would
be saved.

Hope proved to be the truer emotion. At eleven-fifteen,
a distant blur on the horizon slowly grew into a container
ship on a course that would bring her within half a mile of
the raft.

Despite the fact that she sailed under a flag of convenience
and the third officer was Argentinian, he was not in his cabin
but on the bridge and keeping an efficient look-out. He sighted
the raft and instead of ignoring it, reported to the captain.

211

Twenty-Eight

R yan picked up the bottle of champagne out of the
wine cooler, but did not immediately open it. "There's
something we have to talk over."

Laura began to fidget with the belt of her dress.

In his mind, he returned to the moonlit night and the
moment when he'd rolled the seaman over the side of the
Rykonis – another's life taken to save his own. Morally, had
his been the act of a coward or a realist; legally, an act of
murder or of self-defence? Had the detective inspector been
asked, he would have tried to answer and then enumerated
the consequences of the confession. A close brush with
death taught even a dedicated lawyer that the law, in order
to ensure universal justice, might inadvertently provide a
specific injustice and therefore occasionally a man had the
right to deny it the truth . . . Marriage was more demanding
than the law and called for total honesty. "You need to know
that—"

She interrupted him, her voice shrill. "Why can't we forget
everything and just enjoy you being back?"

"Put a cloak over the past to hide it? Sometimes that's
impossible."

"You've got to understand. Just because Keith and I were
so close . . . That doesn't mean—"

"I'm not talking about Keith."

213

"But . . . but aren't you blaming me for everything?"

"Have I been acting as if I were? Of course you encouraged me to do as he wanted. But I understand how he perverted your regard for him in order to persuade you to do just that. I can be certain that if you'd so much as begun to suspect the truth, you'd have told me – however close your relationship with Keith, ours is far deeper."

"I've been so scared that after all the terrible things that happened, you . . . well, suspected me—"

"I hope I'm not that stupid." He looked down at the bottle still in his hand. "I'd better pour before it gets warm." He stripped off the foil, pulled the wire cage free. "I've always wanted to drink Krug to discover if it's as special as reputation has it, but I could never justify the extravagance to myself; now I know that extravagances need to be grabbed at every available opportunity." He eased out the cork, filled two flutes, replaced the bottle in the wine cooler, handed her one glass, sat.

She drank, then said: "Did the police tell you anything fresh when you saw them earlier on?"

"Only that even though they can't yet be certain, they're convinced Keith's fled to one of the countries which doesn't have an extradition treaty with Britain – shades of the story which Captain Samaras fed me to keep me happy! According to Meyer, lacking the proceeds of the insurance swindle to buy essential goodwill, Keith's in for a rough time. In fact . . . I'm afraid you have to fact the fact that you may well not see him again."

"I hope to God I never do!"

He wondered whether now was the moment to do as he had started and confess to her what had happened as the ship began to sink. He experienced a sudden yet deep change of mind. Even in marriage there were, because of the pain their revelation could cause, some secrets better kept hidden.

In his room at county HQ, Detective Chief Superintendent Potter looked up from the report and across his desk at Meyer. "You won't have seen this as it's only just come in. Unsurprisingly, the CPS is negating any action against Ryan. He always evaded rather than deceived, so any prosecution for attempting to pervert the course of justice would be tricky. And after all he's been through, it would be a PR disaster to charge him. So that's that . . . Is there any confirmation of where Tyler's fled to?"

"Not yet."

"Then you must appear to be doing all you can to track him down."

"How exactly do you mean?"

"Good God, man! Do I have to spell things out? Until it is confirmed that he's somewhere where we can't demand his extradition, we must appear to be pulling out all the stops to find him and bring him back for trial. But since it virtually is certain he is, there's no point in actually wasting time and energy looking for him."

"Imitate the CPS. Concentrate on style, not substance."

Potter leaned back in his chair. "There are times, Bill, when your attitude perplexes me."

"I'm sorry about that, sir."

"A senior police officer needs to watch his tongue."

"To show it's not forked, like a politician's . . . It's funny how this case has worked out. I mean, if I hadn't agreed to accept Ryan's word, Tyler wouldn't have had the window of time in which to keep his mouth shut through kidnapping and then the insurance scam would in all probability never have been uncovered . . . Do you remember telling me how wrong I was to accept Ryan's promise?"

"No," snapped Potter, "I don't."

Parker, sitting on the edge of Burrell's desk in the CID general room, said: "Then you really think I ought to tell Mr Ryan that?"

"Of course," Burrell said harshly.

"Even though he's so obviously happy to be back with her that he can't suspect a thing?"

"He's no right to be happy."

"But there can't be any harm in him remaining ignorant since her boyfriend won't be around any more."

"You'd let her get away with it? Making a bloody fool of someone who's trusted her, never doubted her, while all the time she's been kicking him in the crutch?"

"You could be right, I suppose." Parker slid off the desk. He should have had more sense than to put the question to Burrell. And yet, despite the other's bitter sense of vindictiveness, there had to be some reason in what he said. Should deceit and betrayal go unpunished?

"They're all bitches underneath."

Not all. Not Hazel. Even if she was a stubborn bitch and still holding out. He left and went along the corridor to Meyer's room. "Confirmation's just come through as to Tyler's present whereabouts – we can forget extradition . . . It's a funny thing, really. I mean, me suggesting to you the truth about Mrs Ryan and Tyler and you telling me I was talking balls. Do you remember?"

"No, I don't," Meyer snapped, using rank as earlier it had been used on him. When Parker did not leave, he said sharply: "Haven't you any work to do?"

"I've a question I'd like to put to you. My cousin is

something of an amateur genealogist and I was curious enough to ask her to look into Mrs Ryan's antecedents. Know what she found?"

"Not being an amateur genealogist, no."

"Her father was an only child; her mother had a sister and the sister had two daughters, but no son. So she can't have a male cousin. She called Tyler her cousin to explain why he was around so often. That time I called at her place when the BMW was there and like I told you, she looked as if she'd just proved nothing's impossible if you're double jointed – she and Tyler had been flashing the flesh."

"So?"

"What do I do? Do I tell Mr Ryan his wife has never had a male cousin so he can start to work things out for himself?"

Meyer said contemptuously: "Even from you, that's a bloody silly suggestion! Tyler won't be back and so Ryan can enjoy his ignorance, like all the other poor sods of husbands who get a welcoming kiss when they return home from work."

"I suppose that could be right." Parker had said the same thing to Burrell. Two solutions, one of which had to be wrong. He was damned if he knew which one was.